THE
JOURNEY
PRIZE
STORIES

THE
JOURNEY
PRIZE
STORIES

THE BEST OF CANADA'S
NEW BLACK WRITERS

SELECTED BY DAVID CHARIANDY

ESI EDUGYAN

CANISIA LUBRIN

McCLELLAND & STEWART

Library and Archives of Canada Cataloguing in Publication is
available upon request

Published simultaneously in the United States of America.

ISBN: 978-0-7710-4738-1
ebook ISBN: 978-0-7710-4739-8

Cover image: (Abstract shapes) Volanthevist / Getty Images;
(Texture) Pakin Songmor / Getty Images
Cover design: Dylan Browne
Typeset in Janson Text LT Pro by M&S, Toronto

Printed in the United States of America

McClelland & Stewart,
a division of Penguin Random House Canada Limited,
a Penguin Random House Company
www.penguinrandomhouse.ca

1   2   3   4   5   27   26   25   24   23

Penguin
Random House
McCLELLAND & STEWART

ABOUT THE JOURNEY PRIZE STORIES

In the spring of 1988, as McClelland & Stewart was preparing to publish Pulitzer Prize–winner James A. Michener's novel *Journey*, Michener made an unusual request. He asked that the royalties from the Canadian edition of his novel remain in Canada and be used to support writers in the early stages of their career. This generous donation led to the creation of the annual Journey Prize. Now in its thirty-third year, and presented for the twenty-first time in association with Writers' Trust of Canada as the Writers' Trust McClelland & Stewart Journey Prize, the award is given to emerging writers of distinction for a short story or excerpt from a fiction work-in-progress.

As a statement of its own commitment to new writers, McClelland & Stewart undertook to publish the annual associated anthology, *The Journey Prize Stories*. For more than thirty years, *The Journey Prize Stories* has established itself as the most prestigious annual fiction anthology in the country, introducing readers to the next generation of great Canadian writers. It is widely recognized as a who's who of up-and-coming writers, and previous contributors include such now internationally celebrated writers as André Alexis, Sharon Bala, Michael Crummey, Emma Donoghue, Francesca Ekwuyasi, Alicia Elliott, Thomas King, Canisia Lubrin, Yann Martel, Lisa Moore, Heather O'Neill, Eden Robinson, Naben Ruthnum, Souvankham Thammavongsa, Madeleine Thien, M.G. Vassanji, and Alissa York, among many others who have gone on to distinguish themselves with acclaimed novels, short story collections, and literary awards. But we recognize that not all voices are given the same opportunities or heard equally. The Journey Prize commits to amplifying the voices of writers who have historically been marginalized by systemic inequality, including within the publishing ecosystem. This edition of Canada's most acclaimed fiction anthology proudly continues the Journey Prize's tradition of excellence by celebrating the best emerging Black writers in the country.

The anthology comprises a selection from submissions made by the editors of literary magazines and annual anthologies from across the country, who have chosen what, in their view, is the most exciting writing in English by emerging Black writers whom they have published in the past three years. Submissions of previously unpublished stories were also accepted from writers directly.

Beginning with this edition and continuing into future editions, we are making an important change to the Journey Prize: to make the prize more equitable and to further its reach, each writer with a story selected for inclusion in the anthology will be considered a Writers' Trust McClelland & Stewart Journey Prize winner and will receive $1,000. For decades, past contributors have told us that having a story selected for the anthology is the real prize for an emerging writer, giving them the confidence not only to continue to write but also to think of themselves as writers. This change to the prize's structure better aligns with that philosophy, with the prize's mandate of supporting Canadian writers, and with the anthology's aim to spotlight a range of exceptional Canadian literary talent every year. Furthermore, in recognition of the vital role journals play in fostering literary voices, the literary publications that originally published the Journey Prize–winning stories will receive $200 for each story selected for the anthology.

This year the selection jury comprised three internationally acclaimed, multi-award-winning writers:

David Chariandy is the author of *Soucouyant*, which was nominated for eleven literary awards, including the Governor General's Award and the Scotiabank Giller Prize, and *Brother*, nominated for fourteen awards, winning the Rogers Writers' Trust Fiction Prize, the Ethel Wilson Fiction Prize, and the Toronto Book Award. His most recent book is a memoir entitled *I've Been Meaning to Tell You: A Letter to My Daughter*. David lives in Vancouver and teaches literature and creative writing at Simon Fraser University. In 2019, he received the Windham-Campbell Prize for fiction. In 2022, he was elected a fellow of the Academies of Arts, Humanities, and Sciences of Canada.

Esi Edugyan is the award-winning and internationally bestselling author of *Washington Black*, a finalist for the Rogers Writers' Trust Fiction Prize and the Man Booker Prize and winner of the Scotiabank Giller Prize; *Half-Blood Blues*, a finalist for the Governor General's Literary Award and the Man Booker Prize and winner of the Scotiabank Giller Prize; and *The Second Life of Samuel Tyne*. She is also the author of *Dreaming of Elsewhere*, which is part of the Kreisel Memorial Lecture Series, and *Out of the Sun: On Race and Storytelling*, the 2021 CBC Massey Lecture. She lives in Victoria, British Columbia.

Canisia Lubrin is a writer, editor, and teacher. Her books include the acclaimed and awards-nominated *Voodoo Hypothesis* and *The Dyzgraph^{x}st*, nominated for ten prizes, finalist for the Trillium and Governor General's awards for English poetry, and winner of the OCM Bocas Prize for Caribbean Literature, the Griffin Poetry Prize, and the Derek Walcott Prize. Lubrin was also awarded the 2021 Joseph Stauffer Prize in literature by the Canada Council for the Arts. Poetry editor at McClelland & Stewart, she is the Creative Writing MFA Coordinator in the School of English and Theatre Studies at the University of Guelph. In 2021, she was awarded a Windham-Campbell prize for poetry. Lubrin's debut work of fiction is *Code Noir: Metamorphoses*.

The jury read a total of eighty-seven submissions without knowing the names of the authors or, where applicable, those of the publications in which the stories originally appeared. McClelland & Stewart would like to thank the jury for their efforts in selecting this year's anthology.

McClelland & Stewart would also like to acknowledge the continuing enthusiastic support of writers, literary editors, and the public in the common celebration of new and emerging voices in Canadian fiction.

For more information about *The Journey Prize Stories*, please visit www.facebook.com/TheJourney Prize.

CONTENTS

TÉA MUTONJI

THE PHOTOGRAPHER'S WIFE

I met him at a poetry reading. He didn't strike me as someone particularly interesting. I forgot about him until weeks later, when he tagged me in a series of photographs he had taken. I didn't recognize myself in them, but I wanted to. It took me a month to respond to his dozen DMs. I asked if he would take more photographs of me. Not in a "draw me like one of your French girls" sort of way. I just wanted more evidence that I exist. He said he'd be happy to book a session with me, and then he asked me out on a coffee date. And then a week later, instead of sending a price list for the booking, he asked me to join him on a walk. I stood him up three times but on the fourth time,

I called. That's how we started. Every night, we'd get on the phone and trade meaningless details about our days. He often met with some guy who hated women and ran anti-abortion rallies around the city. He did it to have adult conversations about why this man was wrong and why he, as a feminist, was basically the Messiah. He told me he was doing his part.

Don't you think you'd make better use of your time by, like, volunteering maybe, for a women's shelter? Maybe you could offer free photographs? Help them make a LinkedIn or something.

Listen, he said, maybe I won't get through to him. But at least he'll know that someone cares even to challenge him.

Online, I was falling in love with his Facebook posts. They were filled with Hot Takes and progressive commentary on the state of the world. They were about minorities, marginalized people, Black women being the most vulnerable people in society. He wrote about communication being key for healthy relationships, about the importance of having those hard conversations, about fear as a mind-killer, about honing your authentic self. Protect Black women at all costs, he had written. I understand that I'm white but I'm a working-class refugee, he'd commented as a rebuttal. On our first date, I caught him staring at me from across the bar. He winked. When he came back, he told me he wanted love like in the movies. Cameron Crowe and Noah Baumbach were two of his favourites.

Have you watched *Vanilla Sky*? He asked.

Outside at the intersection, I was admiring how tall he was. He stretched both of our arms like that scene in *Titanic*, where Rose is pretending to be Jesus on a cross, except that in our version, we were both gods. It was snowing. I could feel his bulge pressing against my ass, even through both our winter coats. It was the most romantic thing I had ever experienced in my entire life.

~⌣~

The first time we had sex was on Christmas Day. I spent my holiday house-sitting for a rich family on vacation. He was visiting his parents and masturbating in his childhood bed. I remember I was doing the dishes, while also pretending to moan, thinking about how sex is more than the actual act, the penetration. We did it a couple more times over the phone before our first official date. I felt really bad about it so I told him we should take it slow. Perhaps not fuck tonight, even if we're both extremely drunk.

I said, I have no self-control after too many tequila shots, promise me.

We had sex on our first date anyways.

He fell asleep and I sat on his bathroom floor judging myself for it. I didn't feel pressured or anything like that. I mean there was consent and all that. I just couldn't shake the feeling that this person would never take me seriously. That he'd always look at me like the girl he'd fucked on the phone, and then IRL immediately after. The sex wasn't even an in-the-heat-of-the-moment kind of thing. He was naked in bed. I was putting on my pajamas, folding my clothes in my overnight bag.

He said, You're actually getting dressed? I thought you said you sleep naked.

I also said we shouldn't have sex tonight.

He laughed. We can still appreciate each other, though.

He didn't use a condom. I didn't care because I had an IUD, but I had never had sex with someone who doesn't use a condom without first establishing the seriousness of who we are to each other. So I asked.

He said, We're just being kind.

He was getting close. He pulled my face into his and said, Are you on the pill?

No, I said. Giggling: Are you?

He came inside of me by accident and then asked my opinion on abortion.

I'm a socialist, he clarified. Then he told me about his crazy ex-girlfriend.

~~~

I met his friends on New Year's Eve. They were actors and models and filmmakers, though none of them had tangible credit. I was a poet, yes, but they registered me as my paying gig. Which was that of a waitress. The energy in the room was big and tight and intimate. Like an orgy could break out at any moment. These were people who didn't measure their success based on actual success but, instead, on long philosophical debates about morality. It felt freeing. It felt overwhelming. They were thirty-somethings who saw the world entirely through the comfort of this apartment. The walls were red. There was a karaoke station, a bean-bag chair, and several guitars hanging from a wall. After the kiss, I ran outside to puke.

We hung out a few times after that. He'd ask questions like, Did your parents ever beat you, and what's the worst thing you've experienced as a Black woman? His roommate was also Black so he had a personal relationship with Blackness. I told him about that moment you're alone in a room with someone and they suddenly realize that you're Black. I told him about the horror on their faces, about the second-guessing, about the fear.

He said, Okay, that's not that bad. The kids in my schools had it way worse.

I gave him more stories. More moments. More of my days. But then I got frustrated and cried.

He'd say, I see that you're still holding on to the past. You can't heal unless you learn to let go.

Most nights, we'd sit with his friends unpacking a Hollywood movie. Them with their philosophy degrees, me with my double major in English and Literature. I suggested that poets and philosophers use language differently and he told me that I was wrong, language is a matter of facts.

He said, Poets are people who are too scared to face them. In many ways, poets live inside of their delusions. Or, what you call a "metaphor."

~ ~ ~

The afternoon he took my photograph, there was a snowstorm. Neither of us drove and neither of us could afford a taxi, so instead we walked in the slush and by the time we got to the studio, it was locked.

You don't have keys?

It's a public gallery. It's usually open. I bring all my clients here.

I thought you had a studio.

He launched his arms like an eagle, this entire city is my studio. Come on, I know another place.

Maybe we should reschedule? I don't know. I thought you had a studio. I don't do well in the cold.

Jesus, baby, how long have you been in Canada!

He kissed me on the forehead and then took me to the TIFF LightBox, where we were both members. He watched independent and art films looking for the thesis. I watched foreign films for the experience. I was drawn to the grandeur of cinéma vérité.

We shot in the lounge. I didn't like the audience. I always considered photography to be this intimate practice, not intimate the way sex is, but intimate like crying out for the one you love. In the dark. Like the volta in a poem.

The week before he dumped me, he asked me to list three things I hated about myself and three things I needed to change. We drank the same amount but because he was six foot and I was five foot, only I was drunk. It was like this every night. He had olive eyes, a receding hair-line, hair growing out of his ears and from his chin down. He was just my type. A mix between I-don't-shower and beer-belly-is-the-new-man-bun. He broke mirrors and hung them around his bedroom and called it an instal-lation. And in the morning, from his window, we could hear the Caribbean place across the street blasting Bob Marley. He sang all the lyrics. Once, after sex, he tasted his own cum, said, Delicious. Another time, he told me that I should wear my bonnet to bed. He wanted to make love to me in my natural state. He said, I want to have you in the morning when you're most honest. Of the three things I admitted to hating about myself, I told him I wanted to be loved so bad I could die for it.

Exactly. He said, You think the world hates you. But it's all in your head. The world is so beautiful, I wish you could see that.

He reached over the table, travelled the length of my forearm. I can't be the one to make you happy, you know that right?

I didn't remember asking. But still, I said, You're right, I'm sorry.

That's when the breakup happened. We were at the Red Room in Kensington Market. I was drunk, he had ordered me several rounds of shots and had taken none himself. He told me that the kind of work I had to do on myself was beyond his years. It's the way you see the world. He said, I've already reached the point of self-actualization and I don't think it would be fair to subject myself to your journey. I don't mean to be crass, I'm just trying to protect my energy. We just see the world differently. You're dark, you live in a state of perpetual fear, you cry too easily. The more you apologize, the more I think you want me to absolve you of your problems. From the guilt you feel for putting all of your pain onto me.

I interrupted him then. You're breaking up with me? I said.

Yes.

I didn't even know we were a thing.

He waved the waitress over.

Like, I thought that was just sex. Like, all we do is have sex and watch movies with your friends! Like, you made me watch *Green Book* on Valentine's Day. How was I to know you cared about me?

I didn't make you do anything you didn't want to. See, this is exactly what I mean. You catastrophize everything. I don't consent to this conversation.

You made me watch fucking *Green Book*!

Look, don't get abrasive. This wasn't an easy decision for me. But like, if it looks like a duck and it quacks like a duck, then it's a duck.

He left.

I sent four long text messages. He replied twenty-five hours later explaining that he couldn't give me closure, that my healing wasn't his responsibility, that it would be a betrayal to his person to hear what I had to say, to listen to the ways in which he hurt me.

He said, You don't get to claim I hurt you just because you're sad. I said, Okay, you're right, I'm sorry.

He told me I broke his trust by overtexting him without his consent. I said, I understand, I'm sorry.

We agreed that we could still be friends.

~⌒⌒⌐

The following month, he began telling me about his Tinder dates and the women he'd go home with after an event. He was the photographer and they were the clients, the women from fetlife.com. He had a generous list of conquests and I would store them accordingly: the girl who lay there like a starfish, the girl who wouldn't leave his apartment after the fact, the girl who cried about her ex. I felt humiliated hearing these stories. I recognized myself in each of them. They were separate parts of me, which I understood was probably easier than being with one person who is all of these things at once: numb, lonely, and in pain. He said, I'd really like to fuck a girl with a hijab next.

I sent him a text: So is that what you want? You want me to lay there and play dead? We can do that, if that's what you want.

He read my text immediately but replied the next morning: Every time you break my boundaries, you lose my trust. Friends don't fuck friends.

You're right. I'm sorry. I got confused. Can we talk about it over lunch?

Over a plate of calamari, he told me about his latest, the singer-songwriter. They were friends but he couldn't resist, he just had to have her. She sounded and looked boring. Mediocre, regular even. And that's what made her so special. That's what made her at once beautiful and talented. There was nothing to see. So you could be in the audience, comfortable, and non-complicit. There was no show. There was no magic. She was just a person, open and alive.

He told me that he came on her ass.

I thought you said you didn't sleep with friends?

No, yeah, no, it's different. You were my girlfriend.

So weird hearing you say that. I've always wanted to be someone's girlfriend. Like, with the title. I just always thought it came with a proposal, you know?

He didn't respond so I persisted: It's just weird to have been something for someone and not know it, you know?

I get that. He said, It's like those guys you dated. They probably don't know you think they abused you.

Yeah, I said.

It wasn't like how it was with you, you know?

Why are you telling me this?

We're friends. Friends tell each other intimate things.

~~~

It went on like this for a year. And then it was over. It happened like all deaths do—abruptly, in the middle of an ordinary Tuesday. For months I returned to the photographs. I'm not sure why. I guess I wanted to see what he saw. He had captured something in me that I thought I had lost. I looked grounded, confident. I looked like someone who didn't need anyone. And for an hour or two, it was enough. I'd fall asleep picturing the singer-songwriter's ass. How he probably slapped it several times, leaving his mark in a way he couldn't do on my skin. How, on her, he would actually appear, a flushed red, and how he probably caressed that spot on her body, over and over again, until there was no more evidence that he'd been there.

JASMINE SEALY

COLLAPSE

Patrice Martin was hunting in Ganthier, one-hour's drive east of Port-au-Prince, when he collapsed onto the rocky earth. He brought his hand to his chest, squeezed his eyes shut, and rolled onto his back. He took three ragged breaths and then let out as loud a yell as he could manage. The sound, high and wheezing, was swept up in the reddish dust of the plains, and carried off. He tried again, but this time no sound came out.

The sun was beginning to set, the sky already dusted with stars. As the light faded, Patrice tried to keep himself conscious by searching for familiar constellations. Next year, his sons would be old enough to hunt and he was already teaching them how to navigate by the night sky, just as his father had taught him. The further north you travel, the higher Polaris looks in the sky. If the moon is new, connect the tips of the crescent and follow that line down to the horizon, that's south. He ran his fingers through the dirt at his side, grasping at the sparse roots. He closed his eyes.

Patrice's cousin, Arnold, who was also his best friend, was nearby but out of sight, tracking a flock of guinea fowl across the dry, treeless expanse of what was once a virgin mahogany forest. The birds had taken cover in the brush, all except for one, which remained out in the open, pecking at the clayish dirt, its black-and-white wings splayed. Arnold kept it in his sight, edging forward at a crouch. A cry echoed across the valley and the bird took flight. Arnold raised his head and looked for the source of the sound. Likely the shrill call of a red-tailed hawk. By the time he looked back through his scope, the guinea fowl was gone.

"Tonère," he mumbled, rising to go in search of his cousin. He walked slowly, the craggy grasslands uneven beneath his feet. In the distance, Lake Azuéi shone blue, its shores dotted with cactus and brambles. Just across the border, in the Dominican Republic, at the same latitude, the forests grew thick and lush in a protected park. An aerial view of the two countries showed the border clearly: dark green giving way to brown. The history of a single island, divided. Arnold couldn't bring himself to hate his neighbour, though; they had both been pillaged, their lands plundered, the only difference between them the shape and depth of the scars that remained. Patrice would not agree. "Se yo ki fucking colon yo kounyean," he would say. They're the fucking colonizers now.

Arnold reached his truck without running into his cousin. He would later learn he had walked within twenty metres of where Patrice lay silent, alive, but barely. Arnold climbed into the truck and started the engine, his sweat drying in the AC. He fiddled with the radio but could not find a signal. His phone too was out of range. Bored, he put his seat back as far as he could and closed his eyes. When he woke, close to an hour later, he groaned. The sun had set, and they had a long drive back to Port-au-Prince, which would now have to be done in the dark. Just a week before, Arnold's childhood friend had been kidnapped on that same road. He had been rescued, unharmed, that same day. But still, it was an inconvenience and expense Arnold wished to avoid. He went in search of his cousin once more.

He found him after almost an hour of searching. Arnold fell to his knees beside Patrice. The temperature had dropped and Patrice's skin was cold. But he had a pulse, and this is what Arnold repeated to himself, over and over, as he carried his cousin to the truck. Arnold was the smaller of the two, short and wiry, kept trim by CrossFit and yoga. Patrice was big. He dressed as Père Noël every year for their extended family Christmas dinner. His youngest son, Alex, was still small enough to crawl up his round belly and rub the bald patch at the top of his skull. "Pour la chance," he liked to say. Arnold had to stop every few feet to put his cousin down. Once, with the car in sight, he tripped, and Patrice landed on top of him. Trapped beneath his dying cousin, whose breath was still warm against his cheek, Arnold cried. His tears carried the dust on his cheeks into his mouth. He screamed for help, but there was no one around. He heaved his cousin off his chest and, mumbling apologies through his tears, dragged him by his ankles the rest of the way.

He drove as fast as he dared. The road fell away in places, the wheels of his truck skirting the edges of potholes that would be impossible to get out of without a tow. When they reached Croix-des-Bouquets the traffic became impassible, cars choking the narrow streets. Arnold lay on his horn, his head out the window, his cries lost to the din. In the backseat Patrice stirred, moaning softly, his eyes fluttering awake. "Ou anfom kouzen," Arnold whispered. You're okay, cousin. By the time they made it to the only hospital still open, Hôpital de la Communauté, Patrice was dead.

Later, sitting on a wooden bench outside the emergency room, Arnold called his aunt, Patrice's mother. She spoke loudly, the TV blaring a soap opera in the background. It took several attempts at an explanation before he could bring her to understand what had happened. Once she did, she shrieked, a sound not unlike that a guinea fowl makes when you pierce it somewhere other than the heart. She must have dropped the phone, because the noise grew distant. Arnold hung up, took several breaths, and then called Patrice's wife, Vanessa. The line was busy.

He would later learn his aunt had already called her. Vanessa had been washing dishes at the time, and like her mother-in-law, dropped her phone at the news. It sank into the greasy, sudsy water where it lay for the next four days, until the morning of the funeral, when the dishes were washed by another aunt. After this call, Patrice's mother placed another, to her youngest son, Xavier, who was attending university in Sainte-Foy, Quebec.

Xavier learned of his brother's heart attack at a bar, his arm around a pretty girl from Saguenay he'd been chatting up all evening. He nearly didn't answer his phone, his mother called him too often, but he thought it would impress the girl to hear him speak his native tongue. When he learned of his brother's death, he stumbled off his bar stool and out into the frozen night. He fell to the snow and stayed there, until the girl arrived with his friends in tow and pulled him to his feet. Later, in his dorm room, he made several calls, one of which was to his cousin, Sebastian, in Montreal. Sebastian then called another cousin, who called another, until eventually, by then the next day, the news reached Olivier, Patrice's second cousin once removed, in Vancouver, British Columbia.

Olivier was watching premiere league football on the couch while his girlfriend, Caroline, read a book on the patio. She sat with her feet up on a plant pot, her chair pushed to the farthest corner of the patio to catch the last sliver of sunlight before it dipped behind the building across from theirs. Olivier hung up the phone, taking in the news. He hadn't seen Patrice in years, not since the last time a cousin's wedding had reunited them in Port-au-Prince.

Olivier tried to remember how old Patrice was. No more than forty-five, surely. He had two young children whose names Olivier also could not recall, though he knew their faces from Instagram. Patrice was well-liked in the family, a big jolly guy, always quick to tell a joke, quicker still to laugh at one. He was the kind of guy who knew a little about a lot of things. Always stirring up trouble, inciting debate, telling dirty jokes that embarrassed the granmoun. Olivier felt his loss sharply, a familiar ache. It hurt to think of Haiti, to think of family far away, and Patrice's death drew his attention to that ever-present pain, like pulling a muscle already weakened from previous injury. He glanced at Caroline. Only her legs were visible through the screen door. He considered not telling her about Patrice. Her mood had been restless that day, and he wasn't sure there was anything she could say that would make him feel better. Eventually, though, his pain coalesced into something he could name. This was loneliness, he realized. So, after a few more minutes he said, "Babe. My cousin in Haiti died."

She didn't react right away, stopping first to pick her bookmark up from where it had fallen by her feet. She came in and knelt on the carpet in front of where he sat on the couch, sidling up between his legs. She brought a hand to his cheek. "I'm so sorry, baby. What happened?"

"He had a heart attack while hunting. He was so young. In his forties."

"How horrible." She pulled him in for a hug, and he let his chin rest on her shoulder, breathing in the scent of her. She smelled like cigarette smoke, and faintly of the shampoo they both used. "Which cousin was it?" she asked quietly.

"Patrice."

"Oh . . . Jacqueline's husband?"

"No, that's a different Patrice. This one lives . . . lived in Haiti. He was my second cousin."

"Were you close?"

Olivier pulled out of the embrace, settling back on the couch. Caroline rose and went to the kitchen. "We grew up on the same street," Olivier said. "He was older. I know his younger brother better. But we all used to spend time together when we were kids. He was the nicest guy."

Caroline didn't speak for a while. She rummaged in the fridge, eventually taking out a block of cheddar, which she sliced thickly and ate just like that. "It's hard when these things happen," she said finally, "it's like lightning striking the house next door. It makes life feel so . . . fragile."

Olivier didn't say anything else. He didn't like when she did this, took a real thing and made it abstract. But he didn't want to fight. And Caroline didn't do well with guilt—she'd just end up twisting the situation to make herself the victim anyway. This was unfair of him to think, Olivier knew this. He had been thrown off balance by the news of Patrice's death. Everything in his apartment seemed wrong somehow, like they shouldn't be sitting there, eating cheese, talking about metaphorical tragedies when a real tragedy had just struck. He checked his phone. He was in a group chat on WhatsApp with all of the extended cousins. People had begun to send their condolences and to post old pictures of Patrice. He was in a few of them. Caroline came to sit beside him and he showed her his screen, pointing out all the family members by name and relation. She smiled and rubbed his back, glancing back at her own phone every few minutes. He stopped showing her pictures and began checking flights to Haiti.

"What are you doing?" he asked her, after she'd been quiet for a while.

"Oh, nothing important," she said. "I'm trying to remember this word I heard recently. It was a great word. German, I think. You know when you're walking in a park and there's the official path, but sometimes there's another path nearby, a natural path made from people walking over that spot again and again. You know what I mean? Apparently, there's a word for that. I'm trying to figure out what it is."

"Is this for a crossword or something?" Olivier asked.

"No . . . it was just bothering me."

"Man, these flights are crazy," Olivier said, mostly to himself.

"Flight?" asked Caroline, looking up from her phone.

"Yeah. I'd have to go through Phoenix, then Miami with an overnight. Wouldn't get to Port-au-Prince until Wednesday. I have that shift on Tuesday, but I'll have to miss it."

Caroline looked at him, her eyes squinted. She leaned forward and opened her mouth, as if to say something, then she shook her head and stood up, heading to the bedroom.

"What?" Olivier called out, not following her.

"Nothing. Maybe we've got some miles you can use. Check our Aeroplan account."

Olivier went to the bedroom and stood at the door. Caroline was arranging papers on her desk, organizing them into piles. A gnawing heat began to creep up his spine. His feelings for Caroline always seemed to teeter on the brink of tenderness and annoyance. Sometimes, in the middle of the night, he would roll over to find a stranger beside him and, for a moment, he would forget where he was.

Olivier watched as Caroline tucked a lock of thin blonde hair behind her ear, then licked the tip of one slender finger and used it to page through a stack of files, the movements studied and self-conscious. She had told him once that she had been bullied in high school by a group of girls who would invite her into their circle one week, only to shun her the next. He understood Caroline, recognized the stubborn way she occupied a space, like a dandelion emerging again and again from the same crack in the pavement.

He approached her from behind, cupping her elbows with his palms. He breathed her in, looking at where his fingers pressed into her forearms, her skin flaring red at the slightest touch. "That's not what you were going to say," he said finally.

Caroline sighed, and leaned into his chest. "I was thinking I could come too."

Every now and then they could hear the distant whirring of the SkyTrain and the sounds of rush hour traffic from the busy road a block away. Theirs was a nice apartment, by Vancouver's standards. Second floor, indoor parking. An actual building rather than a split-level of someone else's home. Their life, too, was nice. They made enough money to cover their rent and the occasional night out. They travelled too. Malaysia. Tokyo. San Francisco.

Caroline hated that word "nice." She said he used it too often. "You're always saying so and so is 'nice' and this and that thing are so 'nice', it doesn't mean anything." But Olivier didn't know what else to say. This was how he described Vancouver to his many aunties whenever one of them messaged him on Facebook. They always wanted to know what he was doing, so far away. Why he didn't live in Port-au-Prince or Miami or Quebec like his cousins. "It's nice here," he would say. And when they asked about his girlfriend, this Canadian girl they'd yet to meet, they would say,

"She's a nice girl?" and Olivier would say, "Oui, Tati, très gentille. Very nice." And Caroline would cut her eyes at him, sucking her teeth like he'd taught her to, crawl towards him on the bed and say, "I'll show you how nice I am." He could never bring her to Haiti. The thought was sudden, like one of Caroline's metaphorical lightning strikes. But he couldn't shake it. He knew with his whole body he didn't want her to come.

"Yeah, we'll see what the prices are like," he said.

Caroline nodded, continuing to sort her desk, then said, "I mean, on second thought, do you think it's a good idea?"

"Maybe not," Olivier said, relieved. "You don't speak Creole and there will be so much family there. Plus, the vibe will be weird, with the funeral. It won't really be a vacation."

Caroline froze at the desk for a moment, and then recovered, shuffling the papers with extra vigour. "I meant maybe neither of us should go. We've got Shane and Emily's wedding in Toronto in a few months. And we just had to spend all that money on new brakes."

"I have to go. My cousin died."

"Second cousin."

Olivier laughed, a hollow bark, throwing his hands up and walking back into the living room. Caroline followed him. "You know what I mean," she said. "You'd have to cancel that shift and you could risk pissing off the foreman. You said you like this team and want to work with them again, right? Why jeopardize that?"

"Because my cousin died." He said it louder than he'd intended, enunciating each syllable. Caroline looked at him, and then at the floor, her arms crossed as if to protect herself. She jutted out her chin and wiped at her cheek, though it was dry. "I'm sorry," Olivier said, automatically. "I'm sorry," he said again, with more feeling this time. He pulled her to him. "I didn't mean to yell. I'm just upset, you know. It was so unexpected."

"It's kind of gross to use someone's death as an excuse to be an asshole," Caroline said, sniffing into his T-shirt.

A little while later, they sat together on the sofa and Olivier pulled up the flight search on his phone again. It really was expensive. And he hated layovers. Caroline sat beside him, hunched over her iPad. He figured she was sulking and expected to find her on Facebook, but when he glanced at her screen he saw she was looking at flights too. "What if you went out of Seattle?" she said. "I could drive you down. You'd still have to over-night in Miami but it's a bit cheaper." Olivier lay down on her lap, and she put the iPad down, stroking his hair instead.

"I don't know. Maybe you're right," he said. "I doubt anyone expects me to be there, anyway." Caroline played with his hair for few more moments and then reached for her iPad again. She let out a frus-trated sigh, motioning for him to get up.

"What? Did you find something?" Olivier asked.

"Ugh. No. I just got this ridiculous email from the office. Listen to how passive-aggressive this sounds." She read him the email then, her voice incredulous. She laughed a bit at the end and began typing her response, her nails clicking against the screen.

Olivier sat for a while, thumbing through his phone as more pictures of Patrice poured into the group chat. There was one of the two of them he particularly liked. Olivier looked about fifteen. He was in his Eminem phase then: baggy jeans, white tank top, buzz cut. Patrice was older, late twenties maybe, in jeans and a button-down. They were laughing, their arms around each other. A white chair lay toppled behind them.

They'd been wrestling, Olivier remembered.

He thought of the grass against his skin, the way it was always a little wet even when it hadn't rained—colder than you'd expect for the tropics. Their neighbourhood was in the mountains and in the background you could see the garden, lychee and banana trees the only ones he recognized. He thought of showing Caroline the photograph, then changed his mind. He went to the kitchen. "What do you think about frozen pizza for dinner?" he asked, opening the freezer. He stood for a moment in front of it, letting the cold air dry the tears he didn't know had fallen. He stood until he could no longer remember what he was looking for.

More than a year later, Olivier will fly out of Vancouver airport on an airless August afternoon, the sky an oppressive white, the city choked by wildfire smoke. He will send Caroline a message before the plane takes off, a goodbye crowded with too many exclamation marks, too many emoticons to leave room for any genuine emotion. She won't reply before he turns his phone off, and by the time he lands in Port-au-Prince, he won't remember to check to see if she ever did. He will be picked up by his cousin, one of many cousins who feel like brothers and sisters to him, and driven to his grandmother's house in the mountains. The drive will take them through the capital, that indescribable place, the side of Haiti you see on the news, the place his friends in Canada always picture when he talks about home. They will drive with their windows up through this chaos, the shanties, the garbage, the streets thick with too many humans in too little space.

When they reach the mountains he will take a deep breath that will feel like the first real breath he's taken in a long time. There, he will spend the next three days relearning the names of every tree in the garden, annoying his aunties with his constant questioning. *What is this called? What is it used for?* He will sing songs he thought he'd forgotten the words to, drunk on Barbancourt, his cousins laughing when, in the middle of the night, he lies on his back in the grass and tries to count the stars, always getting lost at fifty and having to start over.

TERESE MASON PIERRE

ENDOWED

J erry waited beneath the underpass for Tre, away from the streetlamp's light. Not many people were out in that part of the city, but he could always take out his phone and pretend to chat if anyone got close. It was cold, really cold, and under any other circumstance, Jerry would have gone down to Tre's apartment in the Junction, but Tre insisted that he pick Jerry up, promised a free dinner for his time—even a ride part of the way to his house. Jerry had agreed, but he was regretting it now. Nina was home alone, and it was getting dark.

Headlights turned the corner. Tre's beat-up Corolla swerved slightly as it headed toward Jerry. It jerked when it stopped. Jerry opened the passenger door and got in. "You're late."

"There was a bomb ting by the Tim's, bro," Tre said as he turned onto Eglinton.

Jerry rolled his eyes, but his lips twitched in a smile. Tre was his most loyal customer. "Really. Did she tell you how cold it is outside?"

Tre kissed his teeth. "You would've forgotten. Don' even lie."

They passed a first, and then a second, set of stoplights. "McDonald's is fine," Jerry said.

". . . don't know how she be wearing yoga pants in November."

"Right there." Jerry pointed to the golden arch, shining over a near-empty parking lot. "She probably has a man, still," Tre said, pulling into the plaza. He opened the driver's door. "You want the usual?"

"Yeah."

Tre left and headed into McDonald's. Jerry scanned the parking lot slowly. There was an older man coming out of a convenience store with a lottery ticket in his hand. He got to his car, lit a cigarette, and drove away.

Jerry reached into his backpack and pulled out a small pouch of white powder. Digging around in the backseat of the car, he found Tre's gym bag. He removed one of Tre's socks and slipped the pouch inside the sock, before returning it to the bag. Jerry looked around the parking lot again—empty this time—and waited for Tre to return. It was Charles's idea to do the exchanges that way: surreptitiously. Jerry thought it trivial, but it wasn't as if he could complain.

A few minutes later, he heard Tre's footsteps approach, and the car door opened, briefly letting in the cold and the sounds of late-night millings about.

Tre handed Jerry a McDonald's bag. Jerry buckled his seat belt. "Let me out at Jane."

"All right. Make sure you sit at the back of the bus, eh?"

Jerry looked at his friend, was about to say he knew that already, but decided against it. Tre returned Jerry's gaze, and Jerry could see an opening behind the man's bloodshot eyes, through which something soft and resilient passed.

"Tell Nina I said hi."

Jerry nodded. He got out at Jane and Eglinton and waited for the westbound bus. When it arrived, he sat at the back and ate his meal. At the bottom of the bag was a small wad of cash covered in plastic wrap, which he didn't take out. Not all of it belonged to him.

—

Their street was quiet. Most homes were sleeping, but a few saw people on their front porches, chatting discreetly, smoke from cigarettes and joints fading into the dark above. Jerry walked up the steps to his duplex, checking the frequently empty mail slot on the side of their dark red front door. He fumbled with his keys—chilled fingers—before letting himself in. Nina was lying on the couch, wearing his old painting T-shirt and basketball shorts. The television was on, but she wasn't watching it.

"Where's Mom?" Jerry asked.

"Working," said Nina.

Jerry kicked off his shoes, placed the McDonald's bag on the side table by the door, and headed into the kitchen to wash his hands. A large, covered platter of Swiss Chalet take-out sat on the counter, untouched, not a hint of condensation on the plastic.

"What's all this for?"

Nina sat up from the couch. "Mom's celebrating. Results came this morning."

Jerry knew she'd been stressing about the blood test for days, wondering how a diagnosis would affect her livelihood, even if it was curable.

"And she's out again?" Jerry said. "Shouldn't she be resting?"

"I know, right?"

"Where's Will?"

"Man, I dunno!" No one knew where their step-father was. As long as he paid the rent.

"Did you do your homework?"

"Of course." She sounded offended.

"Did you eat?"

"Yeah . . . "

"You know you lying. Come eat."

Her face twisted into that scowl of hers, whenever she was about to fight with words. Her moaning always worked on their mom and Will, since she was little, but it didn't work on Jerry. He pushed back. Nina finally stood and walked to the dining room. Jerry opened the container of fries and asked how much she wanted. When she didn't answer, he doled out the food based on how little he thought she'd eaten over the course of the day.

While Nina's food warmed in the microwave, he brought the McDonald's bag downstairs to his low-ceilinged bedroom in the basement. He opened the small wad of cash and peeled off two fifty-dollar bills to keep in his wallet. The rest he put in a locked metal container underneath his unkempt bed.

When Jerry returned, he set Nina's food in front of her, took the bread rolls for himself. While he chewed, he cast his eyes around the room, to see if, somehow, anything had changed in the ten hours he'd been out of the house. The potted plant in the corner needed watering. Too many shoes littered the front of the sliding doors. Will's ashtray, normally on the dining table, was nowhere to be seen.

Jerry turned to Nina. She hadn't moved. "What, you not hungry?"

Nina didn't say anything. She picked up her fork and set it down again.

"Mom'll be fine. She makes good money." He tore another roll in half.

"That's not what I'm concerned about."

"What is it, then?"

She looked away and pursed her lips.

"If you don't tell me, I'll take your fries," Jerry said.

He brought his hand close to her plate, and she slapped it away.

"I got a scholarship," she finally told him.

Jerry's eyes grew wide. "What?" he yelled. "Oh, my God, that's amazing!"

Nina's lips twitched. "I know that."

He raised an eyebrow. "Yeah, you know that! Gimme some." He held his palm out and she slapped it halfheartedly. "That's my girl!"

Nina picked up a fry and bit into it.

"We need to celebrate. We need something fancy. Like an ice cream cake."

"Mom's lactose intolerant."

"Good. It's not for her anyway."

They laughed.

"How much?" he asked.

"Ten thousand."

Jerry mimed falling off his chair. He pressed his hand against his chest, took exaggerated breaths.

They laughed some more.

Nina's smile disappeared first. She took another fry.

Jerry picked at the bread. "Do you not see that this is good news?"

"I guess."

"What?"

Nina looked at her plate. "I don't want to use it."

"What do you mean, you don't want to use it? You're just going to hold on to it?"

Nina looked up at him. "Charles called."

Jerry froze.

"I want to pay him back."

Jerry frowned. "No."

"But it's my fault!"

"Nina, I swear to Christ, we are not having this conversation again." He cursed Charles for calling the house. He knew Jerry's cellphone number. "Just eat your damn fries and pay the school." Why was she like this?

"You won't have to work for him anymore!"

"Don't worry about who I work for. I worked for all kinds of folks, people you don't even know about."

"What if I got a job?"

"You have a job," Jerry said. "Being a student."

Nina pushed her plate aside. It scraped loudly across the wooden table. She didn't meet his gaze.

Jerry stared. "You already got a job, didn't you?"

"I figured you would be mad."

He raised his hands and stared skyward for a moment, before leaning forward. "Do you not hear me when I talk, girl? Am I talking to a wall?"

Nina's voice grew high. "It's small. Tutoring. Six hours a week."

"Six hours where you could be studying."

She leaned back, face disgusted. "Excuse me, I just got a huge-ass scholarship. I think my studying habits are fine."

Jerry wiped his face with his hand. "Look . . . " He didn't know what to add. "Just. Don't."

"It's my life."

"Exactly. Don't screw it up with your running around trying to be like all your friends."

She glared at him. "You don't know what the hell you're talking about."

"Fine. Let me handle the money," Jerry said. "I'm almost a quarter of the way there anyway." He looked at her. "Just . . . just let me take care of you, okay? Let me take care of you."

She stared at him, her eyes darting around his face, as if searching for something. The clock ticked loudly in the living room.

After a while, she said, "A quarter, huh? That's a lot."

He scoffed. "Yeah." He smiled at her. "But don't worry about it. I'll get you whatever you need. Just ask."

She pursed her lips again. This time, she looked out the sliding doors to the yard. But it was dark outside, and Jerry could see his sister's reflection perfectly in the glass.

"You *can* ask, you know," he ventured. "And you don't have to hide shit. Especially shit like a whole-ass scholarship."

"I don't know."

Jerry shook his head, reining in his frustration at the last second. "You're in my business too much."

"You're in my business, too!"

He smiled, and she smiled back, just a little.

She rubbed her temples, running her fingers against the wispy hairs along the perimeter of her forehead. "I just . . . I feel bad."

"Don't. Feel determined. Feel special."

"It's hard. Knowing what happened."

Jerry shrugged. "I saw an opportunity. And if I'm working for Charles for the rest of my life, it doesn't matter. Not as long as you're something."

Nina shifted in her chair.

"Hey," he said. He reached for her hand and held it. She squeezed back. "You can't stay here, you know. I'll be damned if you're my age and still living here. You gotta have that . . . that inter . . . something. That thing where you save money for your kids."

"Intergenerational growth?"

He pointed. "Yeah, yeah, that."

Nina opened her mouth to respond, but he held a finger up. "You don't owe me anything."

She nodded, swallowed hard. After a few seconds, she said, almost hopefully, "But you'll come to me if you need anything, though, right?"

Jerry smirked. "Um. No. If anyone gives you shit, I'mma have Charles call them. You know."

"Like he would!"

He threw a bun at her. "Well, if not him, me."

They looked at each other some moments. Long enough for understanding to pass through them like smoke, but not too long.

"You don't need to," Nina said. "What with my recent endowment." She picked up a napkin and fanned herself like a Southern belle. "I'll get you an Xbox for all your hard work."

He kissed his teeth. "Xbox? Get outta here. PS4."

They laughed.

Charles texted Jerry later that evening. Jerry held his phone tightly in his hand as it buzzed. Once, twice, three times, before it settled. He lay on his back, across the surface of his bed, staring at the popcorn ceiling.

In his mind, he pictured Nina, half a lifetime ago, her hands wrapped around a medal she won for a chess tournament, the only girl among a sea of her lighter-skinned peers. The closer they approached adulthood, the more iridescent she became, and he felt light and heavy at once.

He headed upstairs, the metal lockbox of cash at the bottom of his backpack. Charles was always out somewhere at an ungodly hour, waiting. As Jerry passed the living room, he saw Nina sprawled on the couch, asleep, two textbooks open on the coffee table in front of her. The bright dead colours of the Aquarium Channel splashed onto her face, her slightly parted lips.

He touched his sister's cheek. Her face was warm, her breath warm. And her body rose purposefully and safely as she breathed in sleep, in future. He stared at her for some time. His phone buzzed again.

Before he left, he spotted his jacket folded over the top of a closet door and put it on over his hoodie as he jogged down the front steps. There. Better. A buffer against the wind, which had picked up, it seemed, in the absence of bodies. It was as if the world around him misunderstood its relationship with its inhabitants, and Jerry felt something he couldn't quite articulate. At the end of the street, near the intersection, he could see the familiar blue-and-yellow lights of the bus, and headed toward them.

CHRISTINA COOKE

HOMECOMING

"Hey. It's me." I switch the receiver to my other hand. "It's—hold on." I crane my neck to glimpse the clock above the Departures screen. "It's 5:40 a.m., Vancouver time." I pause, listening to the stillness of my sister's voicemail. "I'm about to board my flight. So, um, guess I'll see you soon, sis." I sigh, no one there to meet my sound. "See you soon," I say again, hanging up.

The little light clicks off as the flight attendant's voice fills the cabin: "The captain has now turned off the 'fasten seatbelt' sign . . . " I stare out the window at the crisp white dents in sunlit clouds. I took out a line of credit for this. I hug my backpack against my chest.

I don't know how I'm going to pay it back. Daddy offered to help, but he's sold the drapes, the couch, the living room table. *Is jus' me one*, he said when I asked. The hallway mirror, the reclining chair—all gone. *Wha mi need all dem someting fo?* It's just him one. My brother's three years dead and my sister's far away, back home. I looked around at the house thinning like the hair on Daddy's head, then told him no. Still a year left in college, I got a student line of credit. I'll pay my own way.

Four hours later, the plane bounces twice, shaking me awake. My seatbelt digs into my hips as the cabin erupts in applause. We made it *clapclap* we're here *clapclap* well done, captain—thank you, thank you.

"Ladies and gentlemen," the flight attendant says, "Air Jamaica is pleased to welcome you to Norman Manley International Airport."

Outside my window, mountains rise in rich green swells against grey sky.

"The local time is 3:40 p.m."

The grass, the mountains beyond—all so green like evergreens in spring. I turn to the woman next to me.

"Are we here?" I ask.

She laughs. "Where else would we be?"

I keep searching as people stand, overhead bins popping open. I'm here, back in Jamaica. I'm *home*. I gaze out the window at the passing trees, bright and rich like Grouse on a clear day. I can't tell the difference anymore. It's all the same green.

"You're Jamaican?" the customs official says.

"Yes."

"What part?" he says, rifling through my birth certificate and passport.

"What part am I Jamaican?" I glance at my arms and chest.

He looks up, adjusting a strap on his vest. "What part of Jamaica are you from?"

"Here," I respond. "Kingston."

It says so on my birth certificate, but he keeps watching me.

"Where do you live now?" he says.

"Canada." Like it says in my passport.

"Why?" he says, still staring. He wants to hear me say it.

"Because that's where my father took our family."

"And your mother?"

I fidget with my backpack. "Dead."

"How?"

"Sickle cell." Like my brother.

"Where?"

"Here!" I exclaim. Exhaling hard, I smooth the front of my shirt to make myself calm. "Sorry. Here, in Kingston. Before we left eleven years ago."

He keeps watching my lips move in proper English, my accent all dried up. He smirks. "Yuh sure is Jamaica yuh come from?" he says, stamping my passport and then signalling to the next person in line.

Walking towards baggage claim, I stuff my passport into my backpack. Behind me, I hear the *stamp-and-swoosh*, *stamp-and-swoosh* of the customs official clearing the line. It doesn't matter how I sound. I know where I'm from. Taking three long strides, I arrive at my carousel. I don't see my sister. She said she'd meet me inside.

"Mek mi help yuh, missus." A porter stands waiting in a black cap and maroon suit, his thin beard speckled grey.

I force a smile. "No thanks, I'm okay."

"Yuh sure?" he says, smiling back.

"Yeah, I'm okay."

"Mek mi help yuh. Cheap! Cheapa dan all dem smaddy dem," he says with a wink.

I glance at the other porters leaning against trolleys by the wall. He reaches out to take my backpack.

"I'm fine," I say again, yanking it away.

"Miss—"

"No."

He laughs me off like I've made an adorable mistake.

"Leave." Glaring at him, I set my face into a hard frown. "Go!"

The other porters chuckle. Smile cracking, he straightens up. He's taller than me, thinner, his arms too short for such a gangly body. I look at his hands, calloused and empty, then wonder if he's ever held a passport. I wonder if in all his years of carrying American bags, British bags, if he's ever packed up and carried his own. My suitcase arrives. He doesn't budge as I lean down and take it off the line.

"Move, please," I murmur, setting it on the ground then drawing up the handle.

He looks at the tag's long ribbon, YVR stamped on its tail—signalling I'm a foreigner, I'm protected, I am the commodity that's been lured here to spend and for him to serve. We both know what he has to say. "Yes, *miss*," he says, swooshing out of my way.

Nearing the exit, I can't hear the noise of Customs

anymore. All I hear are suitcases clacking and the porters laughing as that one crosses the room, rubbing his beard and pretending he doesn't notice them. I touch my face, cheeks bunched in a sly grin, realizing that even though I shouldn't, I was born here so I know I shouldn't, I'm laughing too.

Stepping into the muted daylight beyond the sliding doors, I cough then clutch my chest. The sudden change from air conditioning to humid wind makes me wheeze. Coughing still, I walk to the curb, the crumbling concrete giving way to potholed road. Next to me is a woman in a teal church dress yelling at a man tying suitcases to a car roof with pieces of twine. Across the street is a patty stand with a long, long line, and next to it are men in mesh shirts leaning against a wire fence, blowing smoke through their noses as they puff and puff, and children selling Pepsi and coconut water from beat-up coolers and porters pushing too-full trolleys behind white families, their skin garish against all the black, and next to me a child with black arms and black hair and "Akúa!" and down the sidewalk black and behind me black and I look and I look and "Akúa!" someone's calling my name as I pull my suitcase close, sneezing against the car exhaust and patties baking and peanuts roasting in the pit hitched to the bike parked behind Corollas packed with eight, ten passengers and tour buses boasting AC destined for resorts behind policemen wielding batons *move along move along* as so many people, black, black, the sight of us filling me till bursting. My God, I'm home.

"Akúa!"

Blinking, I turn around, holding my backpack close. Someone honks. "Chile, yuh hearin' me?"

A few feet away, the exit doors slide open, rain clouds reflecting off the clear glass. I could go back. I could get on a plane and say *nevermind*, hiding my birth certificate in a place only I would know. A firm hand grabs my arm and spins me around.

"Akúa," my sister says, "yuh comin' in de car or what?"

My sister. Her hair falls in fat twists to shoulder length, silver hoops dangling from lobes scarred with keloided skin. She's wearing a silver dress bunched up to one side in some style I've never seen. But her face, though, that same face: bushy brows angled high over my same cheeks, nose broad and royal above thick lips. She smiles, her lower lids bunching round her brown eyes like Bryson, like me. She's lost weight.

"You've lost weight," I tell her.

"No," she says. "I've just grown up and stretched out."

"Makes sense," I respond. It's been eleven years. Squaring up to her, I realize we're the same height now. My neck tingles with memories of a childhood spent always looking up. "Is this the part where we do the tearful reunion?" I ask, trying to shake the tense quiet.

She chuckles, pulling me in for a hug. "Still trying to be the funny one."

"Hi," I murmur, smiling into her neck.

She rubs my back then holds me out to get a good look, studying me to see what's different and what stayed the same. I lift up my arms, giving her a clear view of my polo shirt and boot-cut jeans and braids pulled back in a messy bun. I still have a soft pooch that Daddy insists on calling my baby fat. I have two orbs of keloided skin, like Tamika, from when I was twelve and tried to pierce my ears myself. Giving me a proud pat, she pulls my bag to the car.

"What took you so long?" she says.

"Customs." I shrug. "You know how it goes."

"Customs?" she says, closing the car trunk. "But you're Jamaican. Why dem giving yuh trouble?"

"That's a good question," I respond, sliding into the passenger seat. She starts the car as I lay my backpack across my lap. Turning the AC to full blast, she cranes her neck to navigate out of the arrivals lineup.

"Tamika," I murmur, unzipping my bag.

She doesn't hear me. She's too busy honking at a tour bus that cut her off. Riding their bumper, she yells something at them, something snarled and angry, patois weighing her words like layers of lichen. I have no idea what she's saying.

"You have grey hairs," I sputter, staring at the strands dipping in and out of her twists.

Still mad, she leans back into the car then responds to me in patois. I try to hear her, sensing the mood in the vibrations from her to me but not catching the meaning. I rub my ears, feeling like I'm listening through water. I don't know what she's saying. She notices my blank stare then exhales slow, giving herself a minute to let her voice adjust.

"Yes, thank you for reminding me of my age," she says. "Just what every woman wants to hear from her little sister." She flashes her brights in the bus's rear mirror then lets them go.

Am I Jamaican? I couldn't understand her, my own sister born of the same blood. Fiddling with my backpack, I take out the box and hold it flush on my lap. "Tamika, look."

"Look at what?" she says, indicating left but stuck at a red light.

I rub my hand over the dark wood. This box, I know. All this I've seen and heard cry and can still hear his voice, high-pitched and sweet. "Here he is, Tamika." I put the box on her knee. "Here's Bryson. I brought our brother home."

In the few seconds between Tamika seeing the box and the car screeching to a stop, we nearly died. She looked down. She screamed. She jammed on the gas like she was losing all her blood through the soles of her feet, the full weight of her in just those five toes. I'd never seen her so pale. You ever seen that? All her colour—gone. You ever seen a black woman turn *white as a ghost?*

"Stop it," Tamika hisses, her forehead on the steering wheel.

I keep laughing.

"Mi seh stop!" she yells.

The cars behind us keep honking, a few drivers leaning out their windows to yell something dirty as they drive past. We nearly died. The insides of my thighs feel a little moist with something I shouldn't say. I can't help but laugh. Leaning over, I wind up Tamika's window to muffle the sound of their slurs.

"You look like a ghost, you know that?" I settle back into my seat. "A black-white ghost."

We're facing a concrete barricade. Tamika managed to stop before ploughing right through.

"Why didn't you come?" I ask her.

She kisses the lacquered grain of Bryson's box in a gentle *hello*.

"His funeral," I say a little louder. "Why didn't you come?"

Saying nothing, she straightens up the car and pulls into early-afternoon traffic. I called her after he died. She said she was sorry. I couldn't stop crying. She said she was so, so sorry. I asked her when her flight would arrive, that I'd take Daddy's car and pick her up. Static crackled through the phone, punctuating the long silence.

"Daddy would've paid for your ticket," I tell her.

She's as quiet now as she was then, pursing her lips as our mother sometimes would. Daddy made all his plans for our departure after Mummy's death. He said we needed a new start, that it was what our mother wanted. Tamika asked him if he'd crawled into her grave and asked her himself.

"*I* would've paid for your ticket," I murmur.

She laughs. "How?"

I was a freshman. I would've found a way—but I don't bother explaining. Even if I'd bought it, she wouldn't have come. When our father came home with the visas to leave, she barricaded herself in her bedroom and wouldn't come out for three days. She was going to start sixth form right there, at home, like her and Mummy had planned. She'd gotten a scholarship. She'd already called and inquired about the fees for room and board.

"Why?" Daddy yelled, threatening to break down the door.

She wouldn't answer him. All she did was slide her scholarship letter under the door, day after day, the seal on the top waxy and bright. Hampton School for Girls. Our mother went to Hampton so she was going too and that's that. My father emptied the house around her, trying to smoke her out with silence. She sucked the smoke in and turned it back on us all. For eleven years, all I knew of my sister was her voice through the phone. But our brother had died. I thought he'd be enough to bridge this distance I didn't understand.

"Why didn't you come?" I ask again. Still silence, so I ask again, and again, till she turns on the radio and switches to the news. We are sisters, not friends. Our shared blood means there is nothing here to earn, to covet, to lose. We will remain sisters no matter what happens, no matter what we do or don't do or how many years we can withstand being apart. I want to scream but she isn't going to answer me, so I clamp my lips shut against the angry weight of all my questions. She keeps driving, sighing with the relief of knowing I'm due no answers. My sister did not come to my brother's funeral. That's that.

"Where are we going?" I ask her.

As we drive along, I lift my left knee, then my right, feeling my sweaty skin slide all over the pleather car seat. I'm angry and I'm hot. The AC's on full blast and it's starting to rain but I'm still so hot. My pits are soaked and my legs feel slimy and now we're stuck in traffic. People pass us on the sidewalk as we wait behind cars backed up at a slow light.

They're hot too, the pedestrians, as they walk past holding plastic bags and backpacks as shields against the slanting rain. And the drivers in front and beside us wipe condensation from the insides of their windshields, then use the same rag, the same yellow rag to cool their shiny brows. Our skin and the sky all weeping, puddles forming in the dips above collar-bones and potholes in the road and I remember now, I remember how much I hate this city. Kingston can feel so deadening in the afternoon, heat sitting stagnant as though taunting a hurricane to blow it free. I crack a window to catch some breeze, smelling rotting trash and fruit ripening in stalls I can't see. I hate this city, but the scent of sweet sop ripening in downtown heat still makes my stomach moan.

It's always so hot, so we build our banks and schools higher, higher, many-storey buildings stretching into the sky to catch wah breeze. And we zoom too fast down thoroughfares and pick-up-and-run across deadlocked streets and *gogogo* cars honking and people yelling we try to stir the air with the sheer force of our skin.

Beep!Beep! a horn goes in quick succession, implying *Move nuh man!*

Beepbeepbeep! another goes, saying *'xcuse missus, move up a likkle an' mek mi pass?*

Beeeeeeeep! like *Woi! Yuh a try fi kill me? Tek time round dat cawna, sah. Mi dehya.*

Beep beep with every honk of the *beeeep*, Tamika too *beepbeep* announcing, *I'm here.*

I'm here, so don't hit me. *I'm here*, so let me through. *I'm here*, so move up and make space. We continue down the street with the press and pause of traffic. We wait at stoplights and crosswalks, windshield wipers squealing in the rain. We hop over sodden grass and clogged drains, children's school khakis creeping muddy from the hemlines up. We run and we yell and we *beepbeep*, announcing ourselves to the hills and gullies and thickening heat. We are here.

"How much farther?" I ask.

Tamika forces a chuckle. "Impatient like wha."

We continue up, up, passing half-built houses with rebars turned red with rust. I turn to face her, my questions turned splinters burrowing deep into my insides. Leaning over, I kiss her on the cheek. She smiles then tugs on my braids, like she would when we were young. Silence fills the car like smoke, both of us choosing to let the moment pass.

We go then stop then go behind streetlights, the houses spreading farther and farther apart the more we drive. Tamika turns down a side street, pulls off the road, then parks on a green bank. I turn to her. She smiles and then turns the car off.

"Wait, so, we're here?" I ask her.

She chuckles. "Excellent deduction, your highness." Undoing her seatbelt, she slides the lockjaw into the grooves of the steering wheel, then hops out of the car.

I look across the street at a series of houses, green roof then red roof then red roof, the first two with flowers and the third without. "Where are we?" I yell, climbing out of the car. "Where is this?"

"Lawd 'ave mercy," Tamika says. "Do you really not remember?" She grabs her umbrella then crosses the street. "This is our old neighbourhood. I thought you'd want to see our house."

I watch her walk ahead, umbrella spread out against the hot rain. I used to fantasize about coming back, about busting down the door and then laying on the living room rug until the new owners left and my own family came home and we would run around and make all the rooms smell like us again. But now, standing on the side of the road, all I see are plain houses with clogged gutters and a stray cat strolling in between. I can't tell the houses apart. Putting Bryson in my backpack and then zipping it up quick, I follow Tamika up the road till she stops. She turns into the driveway of a one-storey house with faded red shingles above cream-coloured walls, front gate crumpled to one side in a mangled mess. Tamika climbs the stairs as I stand by the metal swing set, watching the wooden seat rock back and forth, back and forth.

"Hello?" I yell.

Tamika disappears around the back of the house.

"Hello?" I call again.

I want to see who lives here, who now calls this place home. Daddy sold the house before we left. It was the only way he could afford to get us all on the plane. I press my forehead against a window to peer inside, but all I can see are red security grills and a white curtain pulled shut. From somewhere inside, I think I hear a soft click, like the sound of a TV being turned off.

"Akúa!" Tamika calls.

I follow her voice to the backyard.

"I don't think they're home," she says.

"You know who lives here?"

She nods. "They let me walk through once, before they pulled up the flowers and gutted the front rooms."

I stare at the windows, wondering if my bedroom is still a bedroom and what colour the walls are now.

"That's where you fell when you were six," Tamika says. She points to a large PVC pipe jutting from the top of the wall and curving down into a concrete slab on the ground.

"You used the pipe as a slide," Tamika says, "which was fine. Saved Mummy and Daddy the trouble of having to expand the swing set. Then one day you fell. I don't remember how, but you fell from the top and landed on your face and knocked out your two front teeth. No one would have cared, except they were your adult teeth. They had just finished coming in." She pokes at my gums. I swat her away. "Mummy put your teeth in milk while I washed out your mouth and Daddy called around for a dentist. It was a Sunday. Do you know how hard it was to find a dentist on a Sunday?"

I stare at the spot where pipe meets ground, concrete giving way to weeds. I remember how upset Daddy was about my teeth, but I don't remember the feeling of falling. All I remember is the pain.

"We should go," Tamika says. "They're not home. We need to leave before the neighbours think we're here to break in."

I gaze up at the house. This is a place that's supposed to mean something, this squat little house with cracked tile stairs.

"Are they fun?" I ask Tamika.

"Hmm?"

"The people who live here. Are they fun?"

"They're a family. This is their house. What does *fun* have to do with it?"

I gaze up at the roof. "I hope they're fun." This is a place that's supposed to be deeper than feeling, stronger than blood. I hope the new family painted the walls orange, or red, and turned the bathroom into a closet and my bedroom into a disco. I hope they have a daughter, or a full-grown son. I hope they do backflips off that pipe that would put my sliding to shame.

"Come on," Tamika says, walking back to the front of the house.

"I'll meet you by the car," I respond.

She nods then continues on. Once she's around the corner, I flip the latch on Bryson's box, opening it just wide enough to slip my hand inside. Daddy kept his room in Canada the same. The posters, the plastic figurines—they're all still there. Running my tongue along my teeth, I sprinkle a few pinches of my brother on the cracked-up concrete. The dresser's still stuffed full of his clothes, the handles covered in dust. It's the only room our father hasn't stripped to the bones. Spitting into my palm, I rub my hands together till his dust makes a soft paste.

"What're you doing?" Tamika says. I hadn't heard

her come back. Glancing over my shoulder, I hold up my hands.

"So you just," she pauses, "*brought him with you?*"

Turning back to face the house, I give her a small shrug. "I put him in my bag. I put my bag on the plane. That's that."

She comes a little closer. I open the box like she might join. She stops and then turns around, standing guard around my privacy to do this thing she doesn't understand. So I wipe him onto the pipe, against the wall, into the grass and dirt and remnants of my old blood. I hope the new family laughs. I hope the new family fights, screaming till hoarse. I hope they mistake these streaks for filth, hosing it off and washing him deep. And when they come laughing, ready to play, I hope my brother grows into thick weeds that will break their fall, bones intact.

DIANAH SMITH

THE PROMISE OF FOREIGN

At school, Teacher ask me to stand beside my desk—all the children eyes on me. Teacher smiling like when I get all my spelling words correct. Lucy and Sweetie smiling too, they already know that I leaving for Foreign soon. Darren not smiling. He probably surprise that Teacher ask me to stand beside my desk 'cause he usually the one that get asked. Teacher ask him to stand beside his desk when he do perfect in spelling, when he get excellent in penmanship, and when he the first to memorize his times tables.

The children sit quiet, looking at Teacher, waiting for the announcement. She tell the whole class that

Miss Theresa coming to Jamaica on Saturday, and that she going to take me back to Foreign when she leave. I stand as straight as I can and puff out my chest, just like I see Darren do all the time when Teacher call his name.

At recess, all the children gather 'round. Cutie give me piece of her bulla cake, Sweetie ask me if I want a bite of her patty, everybody want to know what Foreign like. I don't know nothing 'bout Foreign, but I tell them what I think true: that Foreign have plenty pretty things, that the buildings big and tall, that there's nuff more people than in Jamaica. They all listen like how they listen when Teacher talk. Even Darren.

Mama the only one not talking 'bout Miss Theresa all week. Sometimes when we on the veranda or at the table, I see her looking at me but she don't say nothing. Sometimes it look like she looking at something far away. I follow her eyes but I don't see anything where she looking.

Uncle Jeffrey clean the toilet and the chicken coop without Mama asking. He clear out all the trash from the yard and pick up the overripe mangoes that fall off the tree. He burn the leaf, old tree branches, and rotten fruit in the fire pit. The sweet-smelling smoke curl into the sky. Me and Aunt Joycie use old rags to wash the floor and the tough bristle brush to rub the lemon-smelling polish in the wood. When we finish my knees sore and Aunt Joycie back paining her but we can almost see our faces in the shine.

～⁓

Mama sitting on the edge of the bed with that faraway look in her eyes. She pull the yellow sheet up to my chin and fuss with the kerchief covering my hair. Every time she move, her shadow move on the wall behind her. Is like I have two Mamas in the room with me.

"You coming to bed, Mama?"

She rub her hand over the sheet like she trying to press out a crease. "No honey, I still have plenty things to do before this night done."

Maybe is the dim light but it look like something glistening in Mama eyes.

"You alright, Mama?"

She shake her head like she waking from a dream. "Yes honey, I quite alright. Don't you fret 'bout Mama. You go sleep now. You have a big day tomorrow."

She bend down to kiss me goodnight and I reach up and wrap my arms tight 'round her neck. Her small cross press 'gainst my cheek and my nose fill up with the smell of wood smoke and cooking oil.

That night, I dream Queen Elizabeth come to our street. I don't know anything 'bout Queen Elizabeth. I just see her in the big pictures in the buildings where me and Mama go to answer questions and fill out papers. In my dream, the whole street standing on the road waiting for Queen Elizabeth to pass by: Miss Blossom, Miss Vita, Miss Patsy, Miss Ulalee, Maas Dudley, even Lucy, Sweetie, and Teacher from school. Everybody waving a Jamaican flag. It look like plenty black, green, and gold birds flying over my head.

"Your Majesty, Queen Elizabeth!" shout Miss Blossom as her carriage pass by.

"Greetings from your loyal subjects," shout Miss Patsy.

"But look how her hair pretty!" say Aunt Joycie.

I only see the back of her head. Her long white gloves almost reach her elbows and she twisting her hand from side to side waving at the crowd. As she get closer, she turn her head and it feel like the air get knock out of my belly—is Miss Theresa in the carriage!

"Good afternoon, Miss Jemela!" she say, looking right in my face.

When I turn 'round to tell Mama that is Miss Theresa and not Queen Elizabeth in the carriage, I wake up.

When I open my eyes, Mama not in the bed beside me. I hear pots and pans clanging in the kitchen and then Aunt Joycie voice: "I can't believe the day finally come! It feel like we waiting a long time to see Tessie."

"Too long," say Mama.

"How come Auntie Theresa don't visit us before?" I hear Cousin Icey ask.

"Your Auntie visit before. But you never meet her 'cause you was still in my belly when she come. Mama, you remember how Jemela did kick and fuss and hold on tight to your neck when you did try to bring her to Tessie that first day?"

"I remember," say Mama. "Poor thing frighten."

I don't remember that! I feel bad for fighting Mama.

"How come Jemela don't want to go to her mommy?" Cousin Icey ask.

It feel funny to hear Cousin Icey call Miss Theresa my mommy. Is true, but Mama the one that been raising me since I can remember.

"Is not that she don't want to go," say Aunt Joycie. "Is that she don't remember her. Mama, how old Jemela when Tessie leave for Foreign?"

"If memory serve me correct, Jemela barely three months old when Tessie leave."

When I try and remember Miss Theresa, everything fuzzy and feel far away, like Mama calling me from a dream.

I get out of bed and go to the kitchen. Mama and Aunt Joycie grating sweet potatoes, Cousin Icey helping too. I remember Mama say she was going to make a sweet potato pudding for Miss Theresa. Uncle Jeffrey must have already leave to go and borrow his friend Carlton truck to pick up Miss Theresa from the airport. After I eat my piece of hard-dough bread and drink my tea, Aunt Joycie comb my hair and help me put on clothes that Mama leave out on the sewing table. Aunt Joycie say I must look presentable for when Miss Theresa reach. When Mama see me she say to make sure I don't dirty up my clothes or root up my hair.

I go out to the yard and turn over a wash bucket and sit down. The long flies with the pretty green and blue wings zip 'round the yard and two land on the clothesline in front of me. Their wings shimmer in the sunlight. I wonder if they have green and blue wing flies in Foreign. My school uniform on the clothesline—my white blouse and brown dress, stiff with starch—along with three pairs of Uncle Jeffrey socks, six of his briefs, two of Mama slips and four of her aprons on the line too. Aunt Joycie must have already take down her and Cousin Icey clothes. If Miss Theresa live in Jamaica I wonder if she take down mine and her clothes off the clothesline when they dry. I wonder if she blow my soup if it too hot. I wonder if she comb my hair for school and never comb it too tight. When I come home after school I wonder if she ask me what I learn. I wonder if she sleep next to me at night. I wonder if in the morning she make my breakfast just how I like it and don't force me to eat soft boil eggs.

I don't notice when Cousin Icey come outside until she turn over a bucket and sit down next to me. She wearing her judging clothes and her hair not comb nice like mine. I guess she don't have to look present-able for Miss Theresa.

"How long you think it take Auntie Theresa to fly from Foreign?" she ask.

I know it must take a long time to fly from Foreign, 'cause when anybody come from Foreign, people say how long they wait to see them. "I think it take as much days as school last," I tell Cousin Icey. That seem like a long time.

"How much people you think can carry in one plane?" she ask.

I never see a plane before but I know it must hold plenty people and plenty things, 'cause the big barrels that Miss Theresa send come on a plane.

"Nuff people can carry in one plane. Maybe even all of Clark's Town."

"How much plane you think can fly in the sky one time?" Cousin Icey looking at me, eyes wide, waiting for an answer.

I close my eyes and see a picture in my mind of one plane behind another plane like how cars line up one behind the other on the road.

"As much plane can fly in the sky as cars can drive on the road."

Cousin Icey nod her head. I think maybe she see the picture in her mind of one plane behind the other just like I see.

"But they have to watch out for birds and wasps and mosquitoes in the sky," I explain. "Just like cars have to watch out for goats and donkeys and stray dogs on the road."

"What if Auntie Theresa plane fly through heaven?"

I see Jesus in his long white robe, rope belt, and leather sandals with his hand stretched out to Miss Theresa plane.

A sound like an old man coughing and pots and pans knocking together cut off my answer to Cousin Icey question.

"Auntie Theresa reach!" she shout, jumping up and knocking over the bucket. As she run past the chicken coop the chickens squawk and fly up in the air.

"Praise the Lord, Theresa finally reach!" I hear Aunt Joycie shout from the house.

"Thank you, Jesus! Thank you, Jesus!" shout Mama.

My heart beating hard 'gainst my chest. Miss Theresa reach. Miss Theresa, who everybody talking 'bout all week. Miss Theresa, who send the barrel at Christmas and when school start. Miss Theresa, who taking me back to Foreign with her when she leave.

I walk slow through the back kitchen, through the front room and out the front door to the veranda. Mama standing there wiping her hands on her apron, saying over and over again, "Thank you, Jesus!" I stand beside her and put my two hands on my belly. It feel warm and start to tremble like fireflies flitting 'round inside. It feel like that the first day of Infant School. That morning, Mama dress me in my new uniform, plait my hair in two, and tie two brown ribbons in my hair to match my uniform. When we reach the school,

Mama hug and kiss me and tell me she come back for me when school finish. When I realize she leaving is when the fireflies start to fly really fast in my belly. Before I know what happen, I throw up my hard-dough bread and tea all over the lace-up shoes Miss Theresa send me.

Carlton truck shake and give one loud cough before it finally stop. Uncle Jeffrey jump down from the driver seat, walk 'round to the other side of the truck, and open the door. The first thing I see is a broad beige hat drape over a face, and a gold hoop earring sparkling in the sunlight. Next, a foot in a beige sandal touch the ground; the other foot barely touch the ground before Aunt Joycie loud voice fill up the air.

"Tessie, you reach, you reach, you finally reach!" She grab one of Miss Theresa bags out of her hand.

"Is all right, Joycie, I can manage!" say Miss Theresa.

"Stop you foolishness, you been travelling since morning!"

"Welcome home, Auntie!" say Cousin Icey, pulling on the leg of Miss Theresa pantsuit.

A smile brighten Miss Theresa face. "You must be Little Icey!" she say, stooping and kissing Cousin Icey on her cheek. Cousin Icey smile wide.

Miss Theresa gold bangles slide down her arm and make a tinkling sound as she wave at me and Mama on the veranda. Mama laugh and wave back. Even from the veranda, I can see the gap between Miss Theresa two front teeth. I pass my tongue over my front teeth to see if I can feel a gap. I not sure what to do or say, so I just lean 'gainst Mama. Then I feel Mama hand on my back. "Jemela, go give you mother a hug."

I look up in her face. I want to say, *Can I stay here with you?*

Mama smile down at me. "Is alright, honey, I right here."

I walk slow down the first step. Uncle Jeffrey pass by. He pat me on the head even though he struggling with Miss Theresa bags. I wonder if she get mad if he can't manage and one drop in the dirt by mistake. Aunt Joycie big-woman laugh fill up my ears as I step down the second step. I hear the creak of Maas Dudley rocking chair when I reach the last step. My foot feel heavy, like how people must feel after they get baptize, their white baptizing clothes soak with river water. I know I reach Miss Theresa 'cause I can see gold paint toenails in beige sandals. I try to lift my head but it won't lift. I know Mama watching from the veranda. The sun hot 'gainst the back of my neck. I feel a hand, soft like tissue paper, under my chin, lifting up my head. Shiny eyes blink at me behind long lashes, gold dust sprinkle on the eyebrows and cheeks, a little bit of gold-coloured lipstick smear on the front teeth. Miss Theresa smiling at me like how Mama smile when a neighbour come to the gate that she don't see in a long time.

"Good morning, Miss Jemela," she say in a soft voice that sound like a younger Mama. She pull me 'gainst her and wrap her arms tight 'round my body. A sharp, flowery perfume tickle my nose. The buckle from her belt feel cold 'gainst my cheek. Her hands feel warm on my back. Is this what it like to have my own mama?

LUE PALMER

I SWALLOW CREATURES WHOLE

I lie till my belly feels like it's 'bout to bust. "What's that on your face!?" Mama screaming at me. "What's that in your mouth!?" She got my head tilted back, staring down past my teeth into my throat-hole. She got one eye closed and the other staring wide. My brown throat scratch, and my belly set to rumble.

"Lord, this child been swallowing creatures whole!" she say.

Mama look deep deep down into my belly and see: judges with they white-powdered wigs on, they hooved feet and long fingers scratching for the verdict. She see social workers with pickney sacks, and they crawling

76

limbs that reach into windows to snatch up a baby. She see red and blue sirens, falling deep down into the darkness, they colours calling out and trying to clamber onto the walls. She see this child swallowed up the mayor, he wife, three kids, and the mistress.

Mama looking down my throat-hole at them clamouring for air. And me holding belly rumbling, set to burst.

Mama go to the fridge and take out the ginger ale. She spin it till it flat. She hand me a glass. She kiss the top of my head.

I been swallowing creatures whole.

ZILLA JONES

LADY

The first time I ever saw a man's penis, Rochelle was right there beside me. It was my first penis, but not hers; if she were to be believed, she had seen dozens of them already, even though we were only sixteen. I thought I would be completely entranced by the sight of the male organ snapping out from its owner's underwear, a dark, rigid, pulsing cylinder. But to this day, the name of its owner eludes me and when I remember that moment, I think only of Rochelle.

As I pulled my first penis free of the clinging cotton, I was primarily interested in Rochelle's reaction as to how I was handling it. Following her instructions, I checked it to make sure it didn't have any of the welts or lesions that signaled a sexually transmitted disease, as the school nurse would call it. Nowadays it's considered more correct to say "sexually transmitted infection." But Rochelle put it differently.

"Make sure his dick ain't fuckin' nasty. You don't want some rancid jizz touching you."

Satisfied that it appeared healthy, I bent over the penis to lick the length of it, cradling it between my hands and desperately hoping that I was demonstrating the technique Rochelle had taught me on countless lollipops and bananas.

"You gotta open wide and shove that sucker in," she instructed. "And when he comes, men love it if you swallow."

"Swallow, like, what comes out of it?" I asked, recoiling. It was Rochelle who taught me that "come" had two meanings. "Come" was when a man was sexually stimulated and thick sticky white liquid, called "cum," came shooting out of his penis.

"That's the shit that gets you pregnant, so better in your mouth than your pussy," she explained.

Rochelle taught me a lot of things: how to curse somebody out so that they would never bother you again ("cock-sucking motherfucker of a fucking bastard lily-white boy fucker"); how to dance in a way to get the attention of anyone you wanted at the school dance by drawing circles with your hips to beckon them closer and then grinding your pelvis assertively against theirs; how to change an "F" on your report card to a "B" using a Xerox machine and a pencil; how to steal French fries from the lunch line and tell the cafeteria ladies they were being racist if they tried to stop you.

Rochelle didn't care about the boys, her grades, or anything to do with school. She was fond of proclaiming, "School is a white man's invention to force their ways on us." The only reason she came at all was because her social worker from Child and Family Services got up her ass if she didn't. She never referred to her social worker or her foster parents as Child and Family Services; they were "those fucking people" or "those fucking white people."

I was fascinated by Rochelle from the moment I saw her beside her locker on the first day of grade eleven. There were no other Black girls at West Acres High School, and, unlike me, she was unapologetically and unquestioningly Black. I wore my colour shamefully, doubtingly, shrugging it on like a robe each day, hoping no one would notice it. I crept through the school as an interloper, pretending that if I wore the same clothes and listened to the same music and spoke the same way as my classmates did, I could infiltrate their social circles and become so familiar to them that they would forget that they had called me "poo-face" throughout my elementary school years. I knew that I could never actually be white, but I believed I could still belong—that a lifetime of proximity to whiteness would allow a little of its gloss to rub off on me with its protective glaze.

Rochelle was a revelation. Her hair was sculpted into long thick purple braids that whipped around her head like ropes. She wore a big silver chain with the map of Africa dangling at the end of it and a pair of headphones that hugged her neck like a second necklace and pumped hip-hop music into the air around her. She seemed to have stepped right out of a music video into the hallway.

Watching the new girl from afar, I began to revise my thinking on the subject of my Blackness. I took note of how my classmates were both repelled and fascinated by her. The popular boys spent the day discussing her low-rise baggy jeans that showed the top of her lacy thong underwear, along with the cropped T-shirt that displayed her pierced belly button.

Opinions ranged from "That chick's body is banging" to "I'd do her" to "Her ass is way too big." At some point during our homework time in math class, one of the boys turned to me.

"Hey, Chastity," he said. "You should wear an outfit like that other Black chick."

Instead of taking offence, I burned with pride that I had been compared to someone so earthy, so singular, so radiant. I wished I could wear an outfit like that, but my mother posed a formidable obstacle. My mother, born in Barbados, which she called "Little England," raised me according to the laws laid down by her own mother, and my nana's most sacred belief was that the most important thing a woman could do in her life was be a lady.

Being a lady meant carrying yourself with dignity and grace in the face of whatever trials and tribulations might assail you. A lady never lost her cool. She never swore. She never let anyone see her cry. She kept the things that bothered her to herself, be they a lack of money, menstrual cramps, or past trauma rearing its head. Every day, she covered her dining room table with a clean white tablecloth laid with gold-rimmed china. She used crystal drinking glasses for even a sip of water, wore a slip under her dresses and skirts without fail, and made sure that no one, even the mailman, ever saw her hair uncombed.

My mother once told me about the day her papa's mistress came to the door one Saturday morning. The children were all at home and they surely heard when the mistress told Nana her days were numbered and she, the mistress, would be taking Nana's place very soon. Nana listened politely, then said, "Thank you for coming and telling me this, but I will always be the lady of the house, and my feet are the only ones that will ever go under this table. Goodbye." And she closed the door in the mistress' face.

One of the children quavered, "Is that lady really moving in here?"

Nana replied, "First of all, that woman is not a lady. And no, she is not moving in here, because decent men like your Papa don't want women like that in their houses."

When my mother left Barbados to study in Canada, she knew she would be a lady—a man's wife, not a whore begging for crumbs. But she wanted a man who wouldn't stoop to throwing even crumbs at another woman. No, my mother wanted the whole loaf of her marriage, and she found that in my father, a church pastor from Turks and Caicos, in addition to being an engineer and, later, a professor of engineering. My mother liked to tell how she refused to marry him until he swore to her on his mother's life and three Bibles that he would take his vows seriously. They intended to fill their home with children, but after I was born my mother almost bled to death, and to save her life the doctors had to take her uterus. My mother told this story stoically; if it ever caused her distress, it was one of the many things she pushed down and papered over, as befits a lady.

I put my mother out of my mind when I approached Rochelle after class on that first day of school. She was standing by her locker, openly reaching into her T-shirt to adjust her bra, her headphones emanating a throbbing, dangerous beat.

"Hi," I ventured, dipping my toe into the lake before plunging in.

"Yo! Sister!" She stopped fiddling with her undergarments and turned to face me. It was hard to discern her expression due to the fact that she was wearing sunglasses with saucer-sized lenses, even though we were indoors. "I was waiting for you to check me out."

"I'm Chastity." I extended my hand as I had been taught. "Nice to meet you."

"I'm Rochelle. What the fuck are you giving me your hand for? Do I look like some kinda business guy doing a deal, or whatever the shit they do?"

I snatched my hand back. She surveyed my clothes.

"You do know you Black, right? Because your clothes look like what them Sweet Valley High bitches wear."

The water lapped icily at my ankles as I looked down at my plaid shirt, waffle print T-shirt, and dark skinny jeans.

"You adopted?" she asked next.

"Me? No," I said. "Why?"

"Why? 'Cause just about everyone else in this school is white." She swept an arm around at the sterility of the hallways, their bleached walls and floors and gleaming grey lockers. "So I thought maybe you live with white folks, and you don't look like you got taken into care by them fucking people, which means you're adopted."

"Nope. I live with my folks. Black folk."

"You shitting me!" She whipped the sunglasses off her face to stare at me. She had lovely eyes, a surprising light brown glinting with orange, framed by long, thick, dark lashes. "For real?"

"Yep. My mom's from Barbados and my dad's from Turks and Caicos."

"No fucking way! My mom's from Barbados too. Hey, maybe we're related! Everyone fucks everyone on that fucking island."

In her ladylike way, my mother had often said the same thing. "A lot of people in Barbados are kin but don't realize it, because some of the men are rather promiscuous," she would proclaim, with disdain. "You're better off marrying someone who isn't from Barbados."

I had no intention of marrying anyone from anywhere in the Caribbean. In fact, I wasn't interested in Black men at all—until Rochelle came along.

Rochelle asked, "So where do you all live?"

"On Crescent Street. You?"

"I think it's called Castle Street or some shit like that. Wherever those fucking people live."

"That's a block away from me!" I said. I was still unsure about the reference to "those fucking people," but sensed it wasn't the time to ask.

"You going home now?"

"Yeah." I was supposed to meet Sadie, Jen, and Alice, who had been my friends since kindergarten. We always walked to and from school together. But the thought of another walk filled with their inane chatter about their hockey academy, grunge bands, and our science homework was dwarfed by the intoxicating possibility of spending more time in the company of this perfect creature.

"I gotta go to my locker and get my stuff. I'll come back in a minute," I said, and slipped away.

Sadie was waiting at my locker. As I pulled out my books, I said, "I can't walk with you guys today, Sade."

She wrinkled her nose. "Why not?"

I had not yet learned to assert myself, to place my own desires above wanting to placate others, so I said, "Gonna get extra help for math. It's the first day, and I'm already lost."

"Oh, okay. See you tomorrow morning, then." As she drifted away to find Jen and Alice, I hurried back to Rochelle's locker, terrified that she would have left without me, but she was still there. It occurred to me that maybe she needed me; perhaps she didn't know the way to Castle Street yet, and that possibility gave me courage.

As we started walking, I asked, "Where are your books?"

"Books?" She pulled a face that made me laugh.

"Yeah, for your homework."

"Rochelle don't do homework, chile." Then she added for good measure, "Fuck that." And then, "That's for white people." My parents would certainly disagree with that, but I said nothing, content to match the rhythm of my feet with hers. As we descended the school steps, I saw Sadie's blond head just ahead of us. Sensing movement behind her, she turned to see me with Rochelle.

"I thought you had math," she said.

"Changed my mind," I mumbled, as Rochelle smirked.

So began the politics of walking to school. Sadie, Jen, and Alice continued to call on me in the mornings, and I would evade them when I could to meet Rochelle at the corner. If I couldn't get away early enough, or if she was late and they approached me as I stood there waiting, I would be forced to choose—walk with the friend who was the same colour as me, or the friends I'd had longer. I could never walk with them all at the same time, because Rochelle hated "those white bitches who think they're all that," and Sadie, Jen, and Alice said that Rochelle was "loud." She *was* loud. It was what I liked about her—you might love her, you might hate her, but you would never overlook her.

If there were two people who should never have met, it was my mother and Rochelle. But inevitably, one morning when I was on my way to meet Rochelle, Sadie showed up at my house through habit, having forgotten that I had lied to her the day before about needing to go to school early to work on a project. In the course of a conversation with my mother, Sadie let it slip that I often walked to school with my new friend, Rochelle.

That evening, I thought my mother would have a heart attack as she demanded, "Who is she, Chastity? Why have you never told me about her?" A secret boyfriend would not have caused her as much consternation as a secret female friend. Boyfriends were supposed to be hidden, but there was no reason to conceal a girlfriend unless she was completely unsuitable. Reluctantly, I invited Rochelle to come home with me after school, and she accepted.

I debated whether or not I should ask her to moderate herself, and finally decided against it, as this might just encourage her to be more outrageous. But I need not have worried. Rochelle was on her best behaviour, which for her meant no *f* words and calling my mother "ma'am." But of course, for my mother, this was not nearly enough.

"Who are your parents, Rochelle?" she asked. This was the first important question.

Rochelle scowled. "My mom is Cynthia Deacon."

My mother raised an eyebrow and asked the second important question. "What church do you go to?"

"Used to be Latter Day Saints, but not anymore." I braced myself for the onslaught that would come later, after Rochelle left.

"Chastity says you just moved to Castle Street," my mother continued. I knew she was feeling threatened. We had always been the only Black family living in West Acres, and my mother liked it that way—in fact, it was a point of pride for her. She enjoyed the surprise response she got from people when she threw it into a conversation. *There's this lovely little grocery store just around the corner from my place. Oh, where do I live? Oh, just in West Acres . . .* A lady never bragged. Bragging, of course, was vulgar.

Rochelle scowled again. "Yeah."

"Is that where your mother is living? What does she do?"

"Don't live with my mother." Rochelle scowled. "I live with those people."

My mother pursed her lips. "You live with relatives?"

"No, just people. White people."

My mother's confusion cleared. "Oh! You're in foster care."

I grabbed Rochelle's arm. "I'm going to show her my room," I said.

As soon as Rochelle left, my mother rounded on me. "I don't like her. She's vulgar."

I made a non-committal face. Rochelle had already told me in my room that my mom was batshit crazy, fucking nuts, and also an Oreo—Black on the outside, white on the inside.

My mother went on. "Vulgar, Chastity. You should be able to see that. Those braids! Such an unnatural colour—does she think she's fooling anyone that that's her real hair? And how can anyone believe that Mormon nonsense? And why is she in foster care anyway?"

I was saved by my father, who said it was our Christian duty to be kind to Rochelle. And as I did my Christian duty and walked to school with Rochelle a few days later, she asked me, "Yo! How many brothers have you fucked?"

"Um . . . " I said.

"You do like Black guys, though?" she demanded.

"Um . . . " I said again.

"Girl, you've got to be kidding me!" She shoved me in the ribs, hard. "You've never had a brother? So you've only fucked white boys?"

I decided to be honest. "No, I haven't fucked anybody."

My parents gave me the name Chastity because it exemplified to them everything that a lady should be. I was expected to be a virgin until marriage and then faithful to my husband. I had never really questioned this, but as Rochelle waxed poetic about sex—"when he takes his big fat fucking dick and just pounds it in, that's the shit"—I became curious.

We would have to skip school to accomplish the deed, as there was no way my mother would let me go anywhere with Rochelle, now known only as "that vulgar girl," on evenings or weekends. Rochelle made the arrangements with two guys she knew, friends of her cousin. Not too soon, because I had to practice first. We decided to start with me giving him head, and if that went well, to progress to fucking on a different day.

So there I was, in a North End apartment that smelled of burnt rope, which Rochelle whispered was "chronic," not a white tablecloth in sight, going down on my man while Rochelle did the same to hers, right next to me. The guys were older than us, eighteen or

nineteen. Rochelle had specifically chosen older guys
so that they could buy us booze.

As I checked to see if Rochelle was watching me,
I saw her swigging yet another beer. She burped enthu-
siastically and then returned to pleasuring her partner.

When we were done, the guys invited us into
the living room to watch TV and continue drinking.
Rochelle was already wavering on her feet, her tiger-
coloured eyes glazing over. I had not had nearly as
much to drink as she had, and I watched with amuse-
ment as she stumbled around bumping into things
and then cursing them—"that fucking fuckity table
is getting in my fucking way." But then she dropped
onto the couch as if her legs had just stopped function-
ing, clapped her hands over her face, and began to cry
silently, her shoulders vibrating.

My pleasure melted into anxiety. "Rochelle, what's
up?"

She raised her head. "My fucking mother is a bitch."

"Oh yeah, mine too," I said, squelching any feelings
of disloyalty.

"No, Chastity, for real." Rochelle skewered me
with her leaking eyes. "I wish I had a mom like yours.
She at least cares about you. Mine doesn't give a shit."

Our two companions got up and took their beer with them to the bedroom in silence, leaving the drama to Rochelle and me.

Rochelle said, "Her fucking white guy moved in with us. She thought he was the shit. But he was messing with me almost from the start."

I stared at her in horror. "You mean—"

"I mean fucking me with his skinny, floppy, short pink dick. And when I told her, she said I was lying. Till she caught him in the fucking act! And what do you think she did then?"

"Um, beat the shit out of him?"

"Out of him? Out of me! She called me a little bitch and a cock-sucking whore. That's what I am, see? That's what we all are. They rape our land and then they rape us. All we're good for is to get fucked. You fuck them, or they fuck you. And they think they're doing us a fucking favour when they send us to live with those fucking white people and go to their white fucking schools."

As I watched Rochelle, fearless, feisty Rochelle, curse and cry, the silver pendant shaped like Africa swinging in sympathy across her chest, I realized that she was broken in the same way that my mother was broken.

Rochelle's mother's partner had violated her, while my grandfather had humiliated his wife and children with his casual disregard. Brokenness could be hidden behind the façade of being a lady, or masked with vulgarity, but it would eventually come to the surface.

Rochelle never mentioned that night again, and I was unsure if she even remembered telling me her secret. We remained friends, but her mystique began to wear off. A few weeks later, Child and Family Services moved her to another foster home across town, and she left West Acres High School. She only told me she was going the day before, in the school washroom.

"You're gonna be alone with these fucking people now," she said. I had been alone with them before, so I shrugged. Then she lifted the silver chain over her head and handed it to me. "Just in case you forget who you are again." The map of Africa dangled from my fingers.

"Rochelle," I breathed. "I can't. This is yours, it's—"

"I don't need it anymore. Got it from some mother-fucker, and it just makes me think of him. Take it."

I settled the chain on my chest and looked in the mirror, hoping to see some of Rochelle's poise and swagger looking back at me, however superficial it had turned out to be. I had been alone with these fucking people before, but I hadn't known what I was missing then.

Once Sadie, Jen, and Alice got over their huffiness at having been passed over for Rochelle, they started walking to school with me again, but I no longer allowed them to make their little cracks and digs about rappers and basketball players, or say they were dropping the Cosbys off at the pool when they had to take a shit. One day, a few months after Rochelle left, I cancelled my salon appointment to refresh my relaxer. I watched as the regrowth crept slowly back from my hairline with a mixture of fear and excitement, and I refused to allow my mother to make another appointment for me. The day after I got the straightened hair cut off, I spoke up in history class for the first time, disputing my teacher's account of Canada as a haven for escaped slaves by telling her that Canada had had slavery too.

"I haven't seen that vulgar girl in a while," my mother said, a couple of weeks after Rochelle departed.

"They moved her," I replied.

"Oh. Well, it's probably for the best. I don't think West Acres was the right place for someone in her situation."

Rochelle and I didn't keep in touch. This was before the days of Facebook and Twitter, before text messaging or email, and, as she hadn't given me a phone number, she was untraceable. Sometimes when my kids are in bed or when I'm between meetings at work, I search social media for her, but I never find her. I've had many friends since Rochelle, but I still long to talk to "that vulgar girl," the one who freed me to be a Black woman in West Acres.

A lady bears her own sorrows. A lady never gives up. A lady inspires others. Rochelle was a lady.

IRYN TUSHABE

LUCKY BABOON

The day before fate rendered my mother's tongue silent, I was brushing my teeth after a millet porridge breakfast when she walked up to me and said, "I had a dream last night. There was a bright shining star. I've prayed about it. I think you are the star in my dream."

She limped away before I could find an appropriate spot between clay flowerpots to spit out the toothpaste froth that filled my mouth. All day long at school I wondered what I could have said in response. I told my friend Sarafina and she said mothers, as a group, were dramatic. That they were driven to show their love in the strangest ways.

"So that's what that was, you think?" I asked her. "Love?"

Sarafina said, "They simply can't help themselves!"

My mother's love had felt burdensome, a little cloying even, like on the weekend when she'd hold my face between her palms, saying, "I love you, I love you so very much, my very hard-working monkey," before putting a jerry can in my hands and sending me to the well.

My first childhood home was in Kiyoima, a small hamlet hugging a stretch of grassland, part of Kibale Forest National Park. Tall trees growing toward the sun. A river that doubled its volume in the season of rain so that the roar of its rushing water swallowed all other sounds—the hum of the forest, the cattle grazing in the fields, the shrieking cicadas.

My after-school chore was to sit on the edge of our vegetable garden and scream at olive baboons, sending them back into the jungle. They were by far our most destructive neighbours. They ignored Mama's lifelike scarecrows and uprooted our sweet potatoes and cassava. One day, I fell asleep under the pawpaw tree and Bosco—a stubborn baboon I'd named after a loudmouthed classmate I didn't like so much—snuck past to our kitchen shack and helped himself to our dinner of taro.

"I gave you one task, Lucky," Mama shouted at me in Kinyarwanda, jolting me awake. "One simple job and you couldn't manage it."

I cried. I felt terrible. She was going to have to make dinner all over again, and her rheumatoid arthritis was acting up, inflaming her joints and flooding her with pain. A specialist doctor in Fort Portal had diagnosed her with the autoimmune disorder when she was a few weeks pregnant with me. He suggested an abortion, but my mother wouldn't hear it. She was determined to have me even if it meant pushing me out with her last breath.

My hatred for Bosco multiplied. It wasn't the first time he had gotten me in trouble either. I chased after him, hurling stones and insults alike. "You have an ugly butt and you walk stupid," I yelled. He yawned at me, showing me his sharp canines. I said, "I hope you get caught in a poacher's snare, and that the chimpanzees eat all your children."

Not long after, my family and more than a dozen others were forced to leave Kiyoima. The National

Forestry Authority had reclaimed half the village land, gazetting it for the expansion of the park.

Papa went ahead to Kamwenge, a town an hour away from Kiyoima, to prepare a new home for us.

Months later, as Mama and I departed from the village of my birth to join him, an unusual sight stopped the progress of our rented lorry. Baboons, upwards of thirty, had gathered in the road and were wailing "wa-hoo," a sustained call they often made in times of great distress or when they were trying to regain contact with a lost member of their group. A shirtless man with a hoe slung over his shoulder and a woman with a child strapped to her back watched the scene from a distance, distress writ large on their faces. The lorry driver sounded the horn multiple times but the animals didn't even turn to take one look. Their focus was trained on something in the middle. I sat up, leaned forward over the dash, and saw Bosco lying dead in the middle of the road. Tears welled in my eyes. Had my insults doomed him? Did language possess such power, the kind that ended all moments?

"Bosco!" I flattened the palm of my hand against the dusty windscreen. "Bosco!"

My mother pulled me into her chest and said, "Don't

look." She said, "Think about his life, not his death."

But I'd already looked. I'd seen the blood that coated his lifeless face.

The driver rolled down the window and called out to the farmer with the hoe over his shoulder. "Did you see what happened?"

He had. A speeding vehicle. A couple of baboons had been eating ants in the road, and boom. The male didn't escape in time. The female cried, and within minutes, the others began to come, gathering around the male's carcass.

Opening the passenger door, my mother told me to stay put.

The driver panicked. "Don't go out, madam," he warned. "These animals can be dangerous."

"Stay here," Mama said to me and closed the cab door after she climbed out.

I saw her, through the side mirror, going around to the back of the lorry. She climbed in with difficulty and came out a minute later with a white sheet in her hands. I could see her talking to the shirtless farmer, see him approaching my mother, who held out to him one end of the sheet, which I now realized was a tablecloth. As they cautiously approached the baboons, Mama and the farmer smacked their lips and shook their heads the way baboons did when greeting each other. The grieving animals parted, making a path for Mama and the farmer. When they'd covered Bosco, they lifted his stiff body and carried it to the shade of an acacia tree down in the meadow, the baboons following close behind as in a funeral procession.

When she came back in the lorry, my mother had tears in her eyes. We hardly spoke on the long road to Kamwenge.

We moved into the red-brick house while my father was still building it. The windows and doors were boarded up with iron sheets left over from the roof. The dust got into everything: inside the sugar bowl, between the sheets. I got used to falling asleep while Boulenger's scrub lizards stared at me from their upside-down perches on the naked beams that held up the roof. I failed to get used to the loud soukous music floating from the nearby pub, which remained open late into the night. Mostly, I missed the song of papyrus gonoleks.

Mama took me to a primary school near the railway station, and the headmaster, after asking me a series of multiplications—all of which I got wrong—said I had to

repeat primary five. "Those schools of the bush are use-
less, madam," he told my mother. "The teachers are all
A-level dropouts!" A bushy white beard framed his long
dark face and he reminded me of a colobus monkey. He
swore his school was going to make me smart.

On the way back home, Mama and I walked along
the railroad that skirted Kamwenge Trading Centre,
dividing the shops and markets from the clustered
abodes. I ran ahead of her, making long strides so that
I landed only on the sleepers, my bare feet never touching the jagged ballast. Suddenly I felt vibrations and
stopped leaping. I heard the blast of a distant horn and
my mother, a good distance behind on the dirt path
below, shouted, "Train!"

I jumped down onto the path as the train reared
its head from around the bend. Mama caught up to
me and took my hand. We stood together among the
prickly sword grass and marvelled at the passing passenger train, a loud mechanical snake that rattled on
and on. I'd never seen anything like it before. Neither
had Mama. She'd come to Uganda on a big white lorry
with the letters UNHCR written on the side in big blue
letters. Interahamwe had invaded her home in Rwanda
and bled her parents to death. She'd been to the well to

fetch water and when she returned they lay headless on the compound, their blood seeping into the pounded earth. Horrified, she'd screamed into the approaching nightfall until her church minister came and dragged her away. He bore a machete just like the other Hutu militiamen, but rather than give my mother the death she craved, he lifted her onto the back of his bicycle and pedalled rapidly to the white lorry parked near the church. "Don't look back, Faustin, my child," he told her. Grief and fear tied my mother's tongue. The minister told her to nod if she understood. "Nothing here for you but death."

The lorry brought her and seventy-nine other Tutsi refugees to Rwamwanja Refugee Settlement half a day's walk from Kiyoima. Papa, on a job there two years later, beheld her. He said that her eyes were as the moon tugging at the tides in his heart, and he couldn't believe it when she agreed to marry him. "Me," he said. "A simple brick layer without a shilling to my name."

The last compartment of the train slithered out of view and Mama and I went to the tailors to get me fitted for my school uniform, a milk-white shirt with short sleeves and a blue pinafore dress. She bought me black shoes from a shop that also sold bicycle tires and bags of cement stacked one on top of the other all the way up to the ceiling.

I started at Kamwenge Railway Primary School the following week and was surprised to learn that my classmates didn't know how baboons greeted each other, or how they cough-barked upon seeing unfamiliar humans and low-flying birds of prey that targeted baby baboons. I taught my new classmates a more aggressive baboon vocalization that rangers called a pant-grunt, but which I called "huh-uh" because that's exactly what it sounded like: an inhaled "huh" followed by an exhaled "uh." They'd gathered around me, my new classmates, and I told them that baboons mourned their dead, that they perceived pain and loss in much the same way we did. But after school on Friday when we were walking home, Sarafina, the girl with whom I shared a desk, told me that all of primary five was calling me Lucky Nkobe. *Lucky Baboon.*

"At least stop making the loud baboon noises, eh?" she advised me not unkindly.

I said, "Okay." I missed Bosco so much my eyes grew misty, but Sarafina thought I was crying about the cruelty of our classmates.

"Lucky," she said, "do you want to be best friends?"

We held hands across the tracks to keep from falling off the rails, which we pretended were tightropes.

The night fate rendered my mother's tongue silent, we had said our goodnights and each retired to our bedrooms on opposite ends of the hall. The sound of her voice calling my name stirred me as I was drifting into sleep. I went to her room and she was sitting up in bed, looking much older than she had two hours before. She couldn't move, she said; her legs had stiffened like pitchforks.

"I'll go fetch Papa," I said, knowing he'd be at the soukous pub down the road. He'd been contracted to build a canteen at the health centre and had fallen into the habit of stopping at the pub on his way back from work.

Mama shook her head, no. "He'll be home soon." She wanted a drink of passionfruit juice. There were only two butunda left on the kitchen table. I scraped their yellow insides into a tea mug and topped it up with cold drinking water. She swallowed it all up in one long gulp and said, "Back to bed now. I'll call if I need you."

But rather than go back to bed I ran to the pub. The female bartender said my father was out back under the frangipani, and that I needed to go back out and use the side gate. I found him sipping waragi at a red plastic table with four other men, the yellowish light of the lantern illuminating their happy faces.

Papa ran to a neighbour, the carpenter, who owned a pickup truck, while I rushed back to Mama. I found her moaning quietly, delirious. She'd broken into a sweat even though her forehead felt cold to my touch.

As Papa and the carpenter struggled to get her into the pickup now parked in our compound, Mama stared intently at me. I could tell she wanted to speak but her tongue seemed stuck to the roof of her mouth. A solitary tear rolled down the side of her face.

I wanted to chase after the vehicle as it sped off, but my feet felt heavy. I felt heavy. And a storm was coming. I prayed to the heavens to give me my mother back, but the black clouds spilled rain.

It was still pouring when I got to the clinic early the next morning. The taro leaf I'd used for an umbrella had been insufficient and I was wet, my school uniform suctioned to my body. Mama lay unmoving between pea-green clinic sheets. She looked peaceful, like she'd come to terms with her own mortality. Her pulse was hollow, floating, and the nurse told me it was the kind known to grace the wrists of those who had bled.

My mother hadn't bled that I knew of, wasn't bleeding now, I didn't think. "My grandparents," I told the nurse, "they're the ones who bled. Not my mother."

The nurse arched her eyebrow. "The doctor thinks the rheumatoid arthritis has gone to your mum's heart," she said. "It's what brought on the heart attack."

I said, "Will she awake?"

"She's in a coma, little darling," the nurse said.

I figured a coma was not a full stop, but merely a break in a long sentence. I'd wait for the next half. I sat on the edge of the bed and held Mama's hand. The incessant patter of rain against the roof kept time.

SARAH KABAMBA

FIELD NOTES ON GRIEF

1. Death doesn't care about time zones.

Mama always told Sifa not to answer the phone at night.

Mama would never answer the phone after midnight, even if she was sitting right by it. Sifa used to count the rings of the phone until it fell silent. She used to count the times family members would call to report deaths. She doesn't remember when she stopped counting.

To Sifa, the ring of the phone sounded the same no matter who was calling. But she swears Mama could tell when it was death calling. She'd freeze at the sound of the phone, pause in whatever she was doing—gutting fish, braiding her hair, frying plantain, telling a story—and just look at the phone with knowing in her eyes. Sometimes Sifa would catch her, in that moment before she picked up the phone, see her cock her head, listen, and then square her shoulders before answering.

What is there left to say—death doesn't care that she's tired of missing people she never got to meet.

2. *Sorrow doesn't care about the seas that separate us*

Baba always told Sifa that she should never tell people bad news until after they've eaten.

She was doing the dishes when the phone rang. It's funny the things the mind remembers—she'd eaten fried plantain that night, could still taste the sweetness on the back of her tongue. She could see the stars in the inky sky through the window above the sink, the water warm on her hands, and the lemon scent of the soap in the air. The tile was cold under her bare feet.

She'd paused when the phone rang, the plate slowly slipped from her hands as she silently counted the rings, the sound echoing in her empty apartment.

Even before she heard the click of the answering machine, and Mama's familiar voice, she knew.

She'd grabbed the phone, cutting off Mama mid-message.

"Mama," Sifa said, her wet fingers grasping the phone tightly.

"Sifa, mtoto wangu," Mama sighed. "Have you eaten yet?"

What is there left to say—death doesn't care that she's tired of carrying tombstones in her chest.

3. The body begins to eat itself within seconds of suffering sorrow.

Mama always told Sifa that grief will eat you out of house and home.

After speaking to Mama, Sifa felt as if her stomach was twisting into itself. She barely made it to the bathroom before her stomach emptied itself of everything she ate before.

Sifa drove to her sister's house, one of Baba's old Lingala CDs playing softly in the car. She sang along, could almost imagine that Baba was beside her, belting out the words the way he always would.

Mireille answered the door. Her daughter, Imani, peeked out from behind her mother's legs.

"Mama Sifa!" she cried out, recognizing her aunt.

Sifa smiled and reached down to swing Imani into her arms. Imani wrapped her small hands around Sifa's neck. Her curly hair tickled Sifa's nose, and she let her eyes close, inhaling the sweet smell of coconut oil.

Imani wriggled in Sifa's embrace, and Sifa raised her head, meeting her sister's eyes.

"I missed my favourite niece," Sifa said.

Mireille smiled. "Your only niece," she said as she stepped back to let Sifa in.

Sifa followed her into the kitchen, still holding Imani. "Have you eaten yet, Dada?" she asked her sister.

What is there left to say—death ignores table manners, passports, borders, doesn't care that no one invites him in.

4. If you let it, grief will kill parts of you.

"You think one of us would have got his height," Mireille laughs.

Sifa stares at the photo of Baba. He always seemed

larger than life, filling rooms with his deep voice, laughter, and never-ending stories.

"Grandpa?" Imani grabs at the photo in Mireille's hand.

"Yes, honey, it's Grandpa." Mireille gently unwraps Imani's fingers from the picture.

Mama, Sifa, and Mireille sit on the floor of the living room, surrounded by photographs, albums, and Imani's toys. A tangle of pillows and blankets are in the corner, where Sifa, Mireille, and Imani had spent the night with Mama, laughing, crying, and sharing memories of Baba.

Sifa leans her head back against the seat of the couch, staring unseeing at the various family photos on the walls of her childhood home.

Imani jumps onto the couch and then slides down beside Mama. "Grandpa gone?" she says.

Mama puts an arm around Imani, her eyes wet.

What is there left to say—death comes and goes as he pleases, doesn't look back at the wreckage left in his wake.

5. Absence will leave you feeling bloated, but you can't live off loss.

Baba always told Sifa that nothing brings people together like weddings, births, or deaths.

In the days following, their home is filled with people looking to comfort Mama. They bring plates, pots, and pans filled with food. They fill the house with crying, laughter, and music.

Several people are gathered in the kitchen, while others are in the living room sitting with Mama, sharing stories about Baba.

In the kitchen, pots simmer on the stove, plates are spread across the island, and the dishwasher hums in the background. Sifa recognizes some of the women from her days in the neighbourhood, others are foreign to her, but she greets them all the same—hugging, kissing their cheeks, calling them "mama" and answering their questions about her dissertation, apartment, and job at the university.

"This one is married to her degree," someone says, chuckling. The kitchen fills with laughter, the women talking over one another and joking with easy familiarity.

One of the women pauses in chopping onions to smile at Sifa. "You make us proud, mtoto. We love hearing about you from your mama." Other women nod and murmur in agreement.

They speak without pretense or malice, and Sifa

feels tears at the corners of her eyes. She closes her eyes and breathes in the smells and sounds around her, the frying of sweet potatoes, the sting of onions, and the cloy of garlic and cinnamon. The chatter and laughter of the women like a long-forgotten song in her ears.

What is there left to say—death will leave you lost and found and lost again.

6. Grief will make you remember and forget all at once.

A few weeks after the funeral, Sifa goes with Mama to return pots, plates, and containers. No one expects them to, and they end up leaving many of the homes they visit with new pots and plates full of food.

There is an older woman, Mama Aline, who Sifa only sees at funerals. She is always there, kikwembe wrapped around her waist, headscarf wrapped tightly around her dark braids, sitting with the other women, crying, or pounding flour in the kitchen.

When they visit, she will not let Sifa and Mama leave until they've eaten something. She fries fish, cooks sombe, okra, and fufu, as she tells them how her husband died. Later, over tea and plantain chips, she shows them pictures of her only son, who lives in London.

When they leave, Mama Aline hugs them, kissing them on both cheeks. "Tutanonana," she says.

As Mama backs out of the parking lot, Sifa looks at the apartment building, sees the light burning through Mama Aline's window, the flutter of her curtain.

She wonders who will call Mama Aline's son when the time comes. What is there left to say—

A.Z. FARAH

PILGRIMAGE

Ayeyo Fanni is lost again. Right in front of Cathy's Kiwi Mart & Smokes Shop. I recognize her green sweater and frail frame against the seductive black-and-white perfume ad in the bus shelter behind her. *Believe in your beauty*, it whispers. She sits patiently on a cold bench, looking down the street. One hand firmly gripping a cane, the other shaking gently in her lap.

When I first met her at the bus stop, a week ago, I worried she had been in the cold too long and was getting hypothermia. But coming closer, I noticed that only one hand trembled.

"Just one of those things about getting old," she told me.

She sits there alone again today. Her heavy-knit cardigan envelops her body like a hand-me-down: the cuffs are frayed, the elbows patched, and it is altogether too thin for December.

It had been a quiet morning of paperwork and office chatter, client notes and follow-up meetings.

"Did you hear?" asks Chris, who sits at the desk beside mine.

"What?" I ask, turning away from the window.

"Word has it that Tina is trying to fire Chike."

"Why?"

"This is where it gets good," he whispers. "Chike is sleeping with Toni and you know how Tina loves Toni."

"Lord! Don't you people have anything better to do with your days than to gossip and gossip?"

"Don't act above it, you love it."

I turn back to the window. Ayeyo Fanni is still sitting on the bench. I watch her shift and stir, one hand leaning against her cane and the other on her hip as if to hold herself up, the dusty snow thawing under her feet. Now and then, she looks down the street, leaning out to get a better look at the approaching traffic.

"Shit," I say too loud, startling Chris.

"What? It was just some juicy gossip. So cranky today."

"No. Sorry. Ayeyo Fanni is lost."

"Who?"

"The old Somali lady I helped home last week," I say, pointing at the bus stop across the street.

"Oh, yeah."

We sit there, looking out the window.

"You know her?" Chris asks.

"Not really. Just from last week."

Ayeyo Fanni stands up slowly and walks over to the curb, leaning heavily on her cane. She looks down the street hopefully. Parliament Street is busy and loud, and she seems even smaller next to the surge of traffic. The bus is coming.

"Shit, shit, shit. She's about to get on the bus." I grab my coat. "Please cover for me? I won't be long."

"No worries, nothing going on here."

I run down the stairs and out the door in time to see the bus speed up the street. Standing in the doorway for a moment, I watch the back of the bus. The sign on the back reads Not in Service. I look across the street at a puzzled Ayeyo Fanni, who turns around slowly and sits down on the bench again. I wish I could have a smoke. Instead, I put on my coat and make my way toward her.

When I get to the other side, Ayeyo Fanni is looking up the street with a scowl. Her long dira is wet
from the little puddles the bus splashed at her. Winter
is hard in this place. It has mood swings and demands
layering, toques, and heavy shoes with grip. It is not a
place for the soft cotton freedom of a dira and sandals.

Ayeyo's feet are getting wet because she has worn
her sandals today, and her thick socks are drenched.
Her heavy sweater still lets in the wind and she shivers.

"Ayeyo, Asalam Alaykum," I say.

She gives me a familiar up-down sour look, starting with my short hair and moving down to my baggy
hoodie and tight jeans. It is a scrutinizing frown I have
become accustomed to from Somali aunties on buses,
on the street, and in stores.

"I'm Mariam Ali, Ayeyo. We met last week," I say
in my rusty Somali. "I helped you home, remember?"

"Don't talk to me like I'm a child," she snaps,
"I remember. Mariam . . . I remember."

I'm not sure she does.

"Great, nice to see you again."

She is not listening to me but scanning for the bus.
She wraps an arm around herself and shivers. I think
her hand is shaking a bit more today.

"Do people work in this country? I stand here and I wait and I wait and nothing," she says to me. "I pay two dollars, you know, like everyone else. That bus just goes right by, hhhmm. I pay." She puts out her hand and shows me the toonie in her palm.

"Oh, that bus wasn't going to stop for anyone," I tell her. "Maybe it was broken."

She gives me that look again, like I crawled out of a gutter. "How is it broken? I saw it go with my own eyes."

"No, not broken." I sigh. I don't speak Somali well enough to explain Not in Service.

"Sometimes they don't stop," I concede. "Ayeyo? Where are you going?"

"Why?" She stares me down.

"Oh, ah. I saw you from my office and I thought, It is cold and I should have my ayeyo over for tea and biscuits." I smile and point across the street. "Please, come in. Warm up and have tea. It will be an honour."

Her sour face softens into a smile.

"Here comes the bus," she says. "Thank you, but I'm going to Medina. Tea another day."

"Oh, Medina?" I ask as the bus pulls over.

"Yes," she says, still smiling.

"Medina?" I press.

Ayeyo Fanni leans forward onto her cane and gets up. As she walks over to the bus it beep-beep-beeps, lowering to help her on.

"Are you sure you don't want to walk home instead? I'm happy to walk with you."

As she gets onto the bus she shoots me that same disgusted look again.

"Asalam Alaykum," Ayeyo says to the bus driver as she puts her toonie in the change box and gets her transfer.

"Good day, ma'am," he replies.

I remain standing on the sidewalk, staring into the dark bus. Now the bus driver looks irritated with me as well.

"Come on. In or out?" he says. "I don't have all day."

"Maybe I'll go to Medina too," I call after Ayeyo Fanni.

"Allah welcomes all," she says.

Allah welcomes all, and the Parliament bus will deliver us there. I had not planned this for my day and think of the work on my desk as I desperately search for my transit pass in my coat pocket. I show it to the frowning bus driver, who closes the doors behind me and speeds away. I get the feeling I won't like where we are going. Despite the long wait, the bus is empty and Ayeyo Fanni sits right at the front. I sit beside her.

"Ayeyo? Where are we going?" I ask again. "Are you meeting someone?"

"What is the matter with you, child? Medina. I told you already."

"Where is it?"

"Don-something station."

"Don Mills?"

"No."

"Donlands? Oh, Medina Masjid?"

"Don't worry, I know where. I'll tell you."

"But—"

"La Ilahi! Are you ever quiet? Do you always ask so many questions? Just sit. I'd like some peace. I'm going to do my tasbih. Okay? I'll tell you when we arrive."

She takes out a long chain of green beads and whispers a prayer as she rolls them between her fingers. The bus is silent but for the hum of her voice and the hum of the engine as we're carried through traffic. An empty iced tea bottle rolls back and forth as we stop and turn, dirt and melted slush running down the aisle.

I take a deep breath. Medina Masjid. I haven't been to a mosque in almost twenty years. Not since I was eleven and Rahma Salem stole my patent leather shoes with silver tassels. One Friday, I anxiously left my new shoes with everyone else's at the entrance, but when I came out, they were gone and I had to borrow the mosque's grimy flip-flops to go home. As I walked into the parking lot, there she was—Rahma Salem, surrounded by a small group of girls, doing a little tap dance in my shoes. Tap, tap, tap.

"Give them back!" I shouted.

"Hey, you like them? My mum bought them for me. Aren't they cute?" Tap, tap, tap. The girls watching laughed.

"Liar! Those are mine. Give them back!"

"My favourite part is the tassels. Look." Tap, tap, tap.

I tackled her.

Took my shoes off her feet and smacked her in the face.

Her friends screamed, "Fight! Fight!" Of course, this brought more screaming children, which drew adults to pull us apart.

Rahma cried like she had done nothing wrong. She claimed I had given her the shoes as a "friendship present." In a hijab, she had one of those pretty cherub faces that the mosque ladies loved.

"Why can't you be more like Rahma?" they always said.

"She doesn't start fights in mosque parking lots," they said. I got a long lecture about how to be a lady and a good Muslim.

"Religion is bullshit, anyway," said my dad.

"Good for you," said my mum. "Those shoes cost good money."

My grandmother said I'd embarrassed her in front of everyone. *Respect your elders and act right. Next time you go to the mosque, say sorry to Rahma and her mother.* I never went back.

The quiet rocking of the bus is calming. I peek over at Ayeyo Fanni praying. Yes, her hand is shaking more today, but she doesn't seem all that lost. Is she okay? She notices me looking at her.

"My hand trembles. Just one of those things about getting old," she says. I nod and smile.

I call work and tell my boss I have a family emergency; I won't be back for a few hours.

"What family?" he asks. "I thought they don't live here?"

"I'll explain when I get back."

I know from last week's encounter with Ayeyo Fanni

that her family is often at Medina Masjid. Perhaps someone will know her there.

The first time I met Ayeyo Fanni, I noticed her because there are not many eighty-something-year-old Somali women out and about in the city, leaning on canes, doing their shopping. I noticed her because she had that way of demanding attention, like my ayeyo did, even in silence; especially in silence.

Last week, I noticed Ayeyo Fanni sitting at the bus stop as I looked out the window on my lunch break. She sat tall and straight even when she leaned against her cane a little, a No Frills grocery bag on the ground beside her.

I noticed her sitting there as I sipped coffee and looked out the window at 2:30 p.m.

I noticed her still sitting there when I left the office early at 4:00 p.m.

It wasn't on my route home, but I had to check why she was sitting there all afternoon. I stood there for a moment, watching her silently.

She was looking up at me too, with a confusion in her eyes that asked, *Do I know you?*

"Asalam Alaykum, Ayeyo," I said, sitting next to her.

She said nothing, just stared at me. A bus came, and people poured out and stomped down the sidewalk. But Ayeyo Fanni stayed seated, continuing to stare at me.

"It's cold," I said. "Ayeyo, are you on your way home?"

She said nothing.

Then a phone started ringing, maybe in her purse? Her pocket? She was startled but didn't move to answer it.

"I think that's yours, in your pocket," I said.

The ringing continued for a long time. After it stopped, there was only the silence of me and Ayeyo Fanni looking at each other again.

"Where do you live, Ayeyo?" I asked. "Do you need help with your grocery bag?"

Ayeyo Fanni just gazed up at me and then slowly turned away to watch the street.

Unsure of what to do, I said, "I'm not stealing, okay? Just looking for the phone, Ayeyo."

I put my hand in the old lady's sweater pocket. She looked down at me doing it and smiled. There were a pair of glasses, a key, and a small cellphone. The missed caller had called several times. Ayeyo Fanni stared out at traffic again while I called her missed caller back.

"Where are you?" said the worried man on the other end.

I took a deep breath. "Hello."

"Who is this? Is my mother okay?"

"Yes, she is okay. She is at the bus stop. She's been here all afternoon."

"Are you Somali?"

"Yes."

"Thank God. Sometimes she forgets things," he said. "She is taking new medication. She walks away sometimes. Never too far. I have kids and a baby at home. I can't leave. Can you walk with her here?"

I gathered up Ayeyo Fanni's shopping bag to walk around the corner to her son's house. It was when I tried to put my scarf around her that she spoke her first words to me.

"Get away from me."

"I was just putting the scarf on you, Ayeyo, it's cold," I said. "Come, we're going home now."

"I have my sweater. I made it myself, you know."

"Yes, it's very pretty, Ayeyo. Come on, let me help you up. That was your son on the phone; he's expecting us home now."

"My son Ali is an imam," she said. Suddenly, she was all chatter. We walked three blocks around the corner and she talked all the way.

"My son Ali is an imam. He has four children. They are very beautiful. I'm hungry. I bought beef for samosas. You like samosas? I don't like his wife. She's bossy. Have you ever been to Mecca? It is the calmest place you will ever be. If you go there, drink water from Zamzam well. It heals everything."

It has been a while since my ayeyo talked to me. Not since she heard the gossip through the family grapevine; this aunty called that aunty.

"Did you hear about Fatuma's daughter?" they asked. "She lives with a woman. Like man and wife."

"No! Shame!" gasped this aunty.

"Shame indeed!" delighted that aunty.

"Shame," said Ayeyo as she hung up the phone after calling to demand the truth.

I didn't have the heart to tell her the truth. I wanted to keep gossiping about our old neighbours and their new scandals, I wanted to call for recipes and hear about which cousin had annoyed her about what now.

—

The bus reaches Castle Frank Station and Ayeyo Fanni gestures for me to follow her as she slowly makes her way to the elevators. The first time I met her, she wasn't so certain of everything.

"I like subways," she says.

We are sitting on a bench on the eastbound platform, waiting for a train. It's early afternoon and there are few people around.

"You know, the first time I was in a car," she says, "I was four or five years old. I remember thinking it was a machine that made the earth move." Ayeyo Fanni smiles. "That's what subways feel like. Youth."

The train arrives and Ayeyo leans on her cane and walks into the car just in time for the doors to close behind us.

"Don't like those doors, though. Does anything work around here?" she asks again.

She sits down and pulls out her prayer beads from her purse once more.

"I know what you think," she says. "All of you. That I don't know what I'm doing." She looks down at her beads, rolling them between her fingers.

"I can't sit in the house all day," she says. "I won't sit in the house all day."

"You don't have to, Ayeyo. You just need someone with you."

"I'm not a child." She turns her beads in her hand and whispers prayers.

It's just after midday prayer at Medina when we arrive and the taxis are lined up outside. Crowds of men mill about in front of the mosque, talking. This is not good. I pull the hood of my jacket over my head for a hijab and hope the length covers my tight jeans enough. Ayeyo Fanni and I make our way through the crowd and some glare disapprovingly at me; some give me that up-down, just-crawled-out-of-a-gutter look.

"I can't go inside," I tell Ayeyo Fanni, but I don't think she is listening.

"Ali?" I hear her call. "Ali?" One-third of the men in front of the mosque turns to us. One of them is her Ali. Tall and scowling, he walks toward us. How could she see him in such a crowd?

"What are you doing here?" he asks.

"I came to pray. Don't talk to me like that."

"How did you get here?" He looks at me with the same panic that he did when I brought his mother home last week.

I shrug. "She was at the bus stop again."

"Why did you bring her here?" he demands.

"Leave the child alone," scolds Ayeyo Fanni. "She was merely respecting her elders, a thing you should try. Now I'm going to pray. Goodbye, child." She smiles at me.

"Goodbye, Ayeyo. Maybe," I hear myself saying, "maybe I can come visit you next week, and we can go for a walk."

"Yes," says Ayeyo. "Call before you come. You have my number. I'm busy, you know. Also tea, I haven't forgotten. I'm coming to tea."

I smile. She walks into Medina, one hand leaning on her cane and the other shaking, holding her prayer beads.

"Asalam Alaykum," I say to Ali.

Turning around, I pull down my hood, light a cigarette, and prepare to make the journey back.

TÉA MUTONJI

PROPERTY OF NEIL

I.

Spring 2012. My first week living alone has Neil written all over it. He was the first boy I had ever had in my bed. My bed, which I mentally owned, which I came home to, night after night as an adult child, which had pillows and a comforter and a matching bedside table that I had paid for. The room and the bed went for $550 a month. It was a room in a house that was falling apart, but I didn't care because it was mine to fall apart in. The cockroaches were mine, the spider webs were mine, the sinkhole driveway was mine—even the sun that hit the window at exactly five o'clock in the afternoon was mine. I always thought I would look back and remember everything as being mine. I left my mother's house believing that nothing in the world could ever hurt me again. Today, I try to hold on to this still. I say it a few times. I shut my eyes, I think of all the things that supposedly belonged to me, all the things that could never cut me, even if they tried—my kitchen, my frying pan, my toothbrush, my breast, my left ass cheek—and all I see is Property of Neil, written in big bold letters. I think of my life before Neil: I am twelve, I am fourteen, I am seventeen, neurotic because the world is round regardless of where you're standing. Now: I am nineteen, I am twenty-four, I will one day be one hundred. The world is squared. We lay down our elbows crushing the pavement, trying to get back up. All this because Neil was round, all this because Neil was squared, all this because Neil was everything I had ever wanted.

Scarborough was small. Everybody who lived here came from somewhere else. We all migrated to the same parks and the same bars and the same waterfront. This is what made it so special: nobody wanted to be alone, or everybody wanted to be alone but only metaphorically speaking. The bar down my street was the bar down everybody's street. And every night, some runaway woman-child found herself doing blow in the bathroom stall, giving an old man directions toward Kennedy Station, crying over a mountain of road-kill. Sometimes, that girl was me. I saw Neil my first night out. Thick brown hair, skin like a caramel cone, shoulders like a treehouse. I was in love with him like a matter of fact.

"If I didn't know any better, I'd think you were stalking me."

"What if I was?" I said, also as a matter of fact.

"What are you drinking? Gin? Vodka? You look like a whiskey girl. Fireball whiskey. You've got that whole wild hair, hysterical mannerism thing going on."

"I like beer."

"Alright, alright. I like a good curveball, let me look at you." Neil cupped my face, signaled the bartender a pitcher, something light and slightly crisp. He led me through a crowd of old men and young men. Only a few women; many little girls. Everything felt sticky and delicate. The combination of sweat and alcohol and youth. We found his friends in a booth in the back room. They cheered when he walked in. He was kind of a prophet. Everyone gathered to hear what he had to say. I didn't like beer. But he had a lump of a belly, so I assumed he liked beer. I squeezed into the booth, glued to him by the hip, drinking the beer quickly, forcing it down my throat.

"Slow down, Champ," he said, putting me in a chokehold and keeping me there. "I haven't stopped thinking of you. I go to sleep and there you are. You have taken possession of my mind, woman. How are you settling? Where have you settled? Have you met Clay? That's my buddy, Clay."

I told him I hadn't to please him. He liked to be heard. He liked to bring people together, always for a celebration, always for the sake of being together. He was notorious for this. Clay, I recognized from the week before when I was visiting the city and getting familiar with its people. Clay was somehow connected to everybody—he worked with at-risk kids, he volunteered at the youth homeless shelter, he sold blow for less than regular street price. In comparison, Neil was eerily beautiful. In that, his beauty could terrify a woman, steal her from herself. He gave Clay a kiss on the cheek, then he leaned forward and gave me a kiss on the mouth. I decided that he was in love with me too.

"I was thinking about what you told me last time."

"About what?"

"That guy—what happened to you in high school."

"Oh."

"I just wanted to say that I feel for you." Neil pressed his thumbs on either side of my forehead. "You're strong and unstoppable—nothing and nobody can touch you. You're a wolf."

"Thanks."

"Say it."

"What?"

"You're a wolf. Say it. I'm a wolf."

"I'm a wolf?"

That night, we stretched out on his bed. His bedroom was smaller than mine, furnished with a desk, a bed, and a miniature window. The floors were possibly carpeted and possibly hardwood. It was impossible to tell under all those books, and the clothes, and the towels he kept so perfectly spread. There was a wall covered with notes and letters he said he wrote. They were each folded in half and pinned shut. Over his bed hung a map of Canada with little red dots to signal places he'd been, or places he thought of being, or just places. Neil told me he'd been in love once and that it was like being locked in a burning vehicle. He had a wonderful smile while he was remembering it. He got naked in front of me as if putting on a show. As if undressing to show me what being in love had done to him. Underneath his left breast he had two large cuts. They might have been from skating, from getting bruised in the rink, but he ignored them and began jerking off. I kneeled in front of him and held him in my mouth. He drew a line on my head and took it from my scalp.

"Want some?"

"I'm alright."

"Are you sure? It's the good kind."

"Clay?"

"How did you know?"

"It's a small town."

"It will make you feel better."

I'm not entirely sure what vibes I must have given to suggest that I had not been better. If this was another story, I would tell you how we met: hotel party, downtown Toronto, lots of cocaine, cocaine on my forehead, and cocaine on his midriff. Then, we kept bumping into each other like a thing of serendipity.

The next morning, I examined the tissue underneath his breast. Of course, we were up all night, avoiding the obvious questions, Where do you work? What did you study? Where do you see yourself in five years? But I learned that Neil was interested in writing, that he had learned to write from composing letters to his previous lover, the burning car lover, and had been interested in philosophy. "I think love is something you can physically feel, not necessarily from touching. We have these micro receptors that allow you to feel the love around. Right now, I can feel you hugging, I can feel you all over. Anyway, writing is like jerking off." I was standing in the room, moisturizing my skin. "You can feel me from all the way there?" Neil dug his index finger into a baggy and stuck it up his nose. He walked over, dug in the bag, then, with that same finger, he dug into me.

He grabbed a contraception box from his dresser and threw it at me as I dressed. "Safety precaution."

"We used a condom."

"Plastic?"

"I'm on the pill."

"Yeah, but you're going to miss it today. When do you usually take it? In the morning? It's already evening." Neil walked over to me, put me in a second chokehold. "Come on, baby."

We lived down a long road from each other, Neil and I, and went walking to my place that evening after we had finished drinking. We saw a man stroking a tree with his arms. It was an odd sight, something like a vivid photograph that had been photoshopped, except it was actually happening. Then, a homeless man came out and showed us his fingers. I could tell he was homeless because he smelt like grass covered in piss. Neil reached out to him, said, "Ted, fucking eh, my man." Reached in his pockets and took out three cigarettes. We had spent the night fucking, then dancing, then snorting. Now we were smoking with a homeless man. He was sticking his tongue out at us.

"People get hungry and eat their own fingers," he said. "Look at this, look at this—see that? All fingers. I got all my fingers. Neil brings around sweet things and doesn't starve. Who's this? Lady with fingers."

Neil wrapped his free hand around my neck. If I had choked and died at that very moment, I would have died happy. "My girl," he said, giving Ted the rest of his cigarettes. A five-dollar bill. "Where's all your fucking money, man? Buy yourself something nice, eh."

I think I was once a weightless body surrounded by weightless bodies, a little push and I'd float. My mother said I am unusual, not what she had hoped for. Not a person who could belong to somebody else. Not hers, certainly not hers.

I saw Neil every night that first week. He sat on the edge of my bed. Asked to hear a poem. Nibbled on my ear. Told me that the world was open and that the world was like an apple pie. "Have you ever stuck your dick in an apple pie. I mean, if you had a dick, I mean." Around his friends, he would look at me from across the room and wink. Pet me on the forehead whenever I said something to impress them. He felt good. Everything about him felt good. He was kind of like a blank canvas. Every day with him was like starting over. I liked it because I needed a lot of starting over. I needed a new chance for all the ones I had blown up. My mother couldn't look at me anymore. I had done something. It didn't matter now—nothing mattered anymore. I was sticking my dick inside of an apple pie.

A month went by and I saw him less. Then, two months went by, and I saw him when he felt like seeing me. Then, three months. Every night was the same. He sat on the mattress, his belly squeamish on the bed-spread. His shorts, always hanging around his waist. He smelled like ice, though his skin was perpetually soft and pink from the booze or from the heat. He spoke hysterically about the puck and the skates, how his face smashed the glass seven times during the game, leaving a smooth finish on his left cheek. I had never been to any of his games, but he recounted them vividly. I'd sit in the corner of the room, or on the porch where we often sat after a long week, and imagined him, lost and slow. I heard he was great, unstoppable on the rink, but something about the way his fingers jazzed made me believe he was probably just messy. He said the impact always got him going and he needed me to relieve some stress. He stressed easily, since his convocation, since the divorce at home, since his dad began sleeping on the sofa. He'd beat himself off to regulate his serotonin levels. He'd tell me shit like this when we were sexting. Always I answered, "Neil, Neil, Neil," and he'd say, "yeah, yeah, yeah." I'd nod and adjust myself to fit where he wanted me, between his legs in a doggy position, knees and arms bent, arched back, ass sticking out. I'd check his rolls to see if he had been hurt. A couple of scratches underneath his nipple. A bruise on his neck. I'd press two fingers and he'd grabbed them, popped them in his mouth, and began to chew. We were sweating. The air conditioning had been broken all spring, now at the end of July, his chest hair glued to my breast.

On my birthday, he came and sang to me. He had a terribly awful singing voice. But he loved to sing. He poured liquor down my throat, stretched in his under-wear, sang a dramatic lullaby. He sat up and cried about dying, said, "When I die, all the shit I have inside of me will boil and I'll explode. It will be a natural death." He talked and talked and talked. When he was done talking, he vomited. I heard him, I always heard him: I'd press my ear to the bathroom door, listening to his groaning. Getting a rush from it. I would help him brush his teeth and he would fall asleep on top of me. I was so happy I wanted to die. The thought wasn't an active or physical one. It was more of a pornographic thought. It stemmed from a place of internal stimula-tion. The more I thought about it, the more aroused I became. I went about my day and waited for Neil to show. When he did, I was certain I was coming closer to death so I fucked him, certain I would die. I would snort another lizard. I would be resurrected.

"Okay, baby, it's time."

Neil gave me the contraception pill and fell asleep. I flushed it down the toilet, took a sleeping pill instead.

My bedroom walls had princess characters printed on them. The princesses looked like dinosaurs or pornstars or firemen. I took a third sleeping pill. Neil tossed awake, sticky from a dream, "Hemingway blew his head with a shotgun."

"Plath burnt her head in an oven."

"Fucked on blow."

"Neil, Neil, Neil."

"Do you miss your mom?"

"No."

In the morning, I woke up, and he was gone. I never saw him again. He might have gone back to his room on the second floor of his parents' house. That's where I believed he took me and kept me, ate pieces of me so as not to eat his own finger. I felt like something was missing. In search of me, I began walking around my house first. Everything in it felt distant from what they were supposed to be. The fridge became a walk-in shower. I'd open it night after night to clean myself, stand in front of it and freeze because I was perpetually hot. I missed him. I stayed awake from missing him—drank a lot from missing him. I even saw Clay, sometimes for the street discount, most times in hopes he would transform into Neil and I could live another day. They both had split opened faces—you could see inside of them by staring directly at their forehead. I even considered fucking Clay to feel Neil inside of me—he was growing inside of me. I could feel him, doing somersaults in my belly. I looked everywhere, behind the park, at the Bluffs, on Highland Creek—Scarborough had become larger overnight. When I looked up, I noticed the sky had disappeared too.

2.

Summer 2013. Maggie and I moved to a sizable apartment on Morningside and Military Trail. There was a large hole in the oven door, so we often ate cereal. We told stories of what might have happened for the oven glass to crack so largely. My favourite scenario: it gave birth to an explosive banana bread that broke through from the inside out. I like to think I was a banana bread who broke out of her mother's house. The faucet in the washroom didn't work, so we brushed our teeth in the kitchen sink. Maggie majored in psychology and neuroscience and said that I had matured emotionally since last spring. When we talked about moving in together, she offered to make our home alcohol-free, but I had gotten better at drinking, and drinking had never been my problem.

Her boyfriend was this tall African God who spoke multiple languages. He fixed everything around the apartment except the open oven. It became symbolic of our friendship. When she couldn't sleep, she'd get in bed with me and I would hold her, I would rock her between my breasts and kiss her behind the ear. I had gotten better at sleeping, but sometimes I hurt myself in my sleep. We needed each other. Not in a way that was desperate or out of bounds or even sexual. It was realizing that loneliness was overwhelming, overtly fetishized, that people who craved it were most susceptible to internal organ failure. It was better to open yourself up to the world.

I worked a serving job that kept me in check. The job was demanding. The people were needy. I got exactly two minutes of solitude per day. It excited me, and it made me crumble. I kept busy by writing. I kept writing so as not to think. I wrote these long poems, wrote about a boy who moves his furniture every Sunday in accordance with the sunset. I once said to him, "Feng shui?" and he replied, "Sanity." I often thought of that boy's mother, but I didn't know why.

I took on a few passing lovers, but the walls of my inside had lost all sensation. Fucking felt like breathing. Breathing felt like nothing. You only know you are breathing because you're not dead. I once brought a lighter to my vagina to see if I'd feel anything. The doctor said it might be PTSD.

Maggie said it might be a lack of arousal. "Maybe you're having a hard time relaxing. David does this thing before we have sex, he gives me a full back massage."

"That sounds like a lot of work. Should sex even be worth that much work? I mean, my introduction to it all was fucked up. I was doomed from the start. I don't remember ever even enjoying it. I remember wanting to, roleplaying myself to. The entire thing is literally overrated."

"You just haven't found the right guy for you— wait, are you doing girls now? You just haven't found the right human for you."

"Do you not watch porn?"

"What?"

"Porn is not what ruined sex. Romantic comedy ruined sex. Nicholas Sparks ruined it. I can absolutely promise you at no point do birds begin to chirp in the middle of sex. Fucking *Titanic*. Sex is literally disgusting and bloody and mostly painful. You don't get an accurate, authentic, organic representation of sex anywhere but in porn. Maybe also on HBO, but less so."

"The sex you're having is hardly considered sex. Do you even want to have sex with any of these people? I worry about you sometimes. That sounds really numbing."

"Was there porn in Shakespeare's time? Romance, courtship, that entire thing was also fucked up back then. Porn's recent. Porn's like reality TV but scripted."

Maggie continued tossing the salad in our kitchenette. She cut slices of cucumbers with such malice I wondered if she had been suffering in silence. "I think David and I will get married. I think he'll propose after graduation."

"You should probably start watching porn to regulate your expectation of all of that."

"You need to go see a doctor." Maggie grabbed my hand, pressed it against hers. "I need my maid of honour to have a working vagina in case I need to pawn you off to one of David's brothers, who are all rich and handsome and probably African royalty."

"I did see a doctor. My vagina's perfect. All psychological."

Everybody outside of our apartment seemed broken. If not broken: poor. You could tell from the ashy elbows or cigarette teeth. Now, loneliness felt foreign. Like something I had to actively reach out for. That's the problem with solitude, I thought, as I was giving myself a time-out, walking around the mall, having just finished drinking a bottle for the sake of drinking. You go out looking for a place to be alone and you find crowded malls and crowded parking lots and movie theatres and resto-bars. You stay home to be alone but you find furniture, casseroles with people's names written on them, televisions, books, magazines. You get so beaten up and that's when it happens. Solitude is that emotional response to the lack thereof. Not a physical space or an abstract thought. You gotta stop looking for it to fall into it. Romance, sex, destruction. I liked drinking by myself. I liked being in a public space having just drunk my water weight. I was fine like this—I was in my head like this. I looked up and Neil was standing in front of me, his thick brown hair, thick as ever—his mouth madly trembling.

"My, my, my," he says, "my, my, my."

Now I'm thinking I'm drunk and hallucinating, that the world is spinning, that my head has just been cracked open, "Neil?"

"My girl," he says.

"You're drunk."

"My girl," he says.

Neil had friends. He had people who loved him. They grouped around us, cheering him on, or I was in such a state, I felt like an animal getting eaten alive by a pack of stupid wolves. Then, I was airlifted by a pack of wolves and went bar to bar until none of us had anything to show for. Until Neil, who had a weak stomach and a large throat, began to vomit on the sidewalk, and then vomit in the parking garage. I had forgotten how bad he was at drinking, how much blow he needed to stay wired, how much discipline he lacked.

Now we're in the backseat of somebody's car, Neil and I, and he pulled a bottle of wine from somewhere, which terrified me, so I reached for the bottle and I drank most of it because I instantly remembered who he was. Then, all I felt was fear. I couldn't remember where the fear came from, but I flinched when he offered himself to me. I tried to remember being terrified of him, but all that I remembered was saying his name repeatedly to anchor myself back to reality, Neil, Neil, Neil.

The car stopped, and he pulled me out on the street. We were alone underneath the moon, and I felt actual solitude for the first time. It was equivalent to getting your blood sucked out of your veins, like a fatigue that was nauseating, like feeling the wind blow through your body, feeling it fuck you from your belly and coming out of your back dimples, feeling the air pass through, knowing that there is a hole in the centre of you, a sick solitude, like you could die from being alone.

I could tell we were on his street. I recognized the elementary school and the cracked trees. The way he held on to me terrified me. But it wasn't the holding that held me in place. It was the fear that if he let go, I would be overcome by vertigo, and I wouldn't wake up from it. He began to kiss me, and I pulled him toward his house. He lifted me slightly, then my back was pressed against a wall. He was going for my neck. He was going for my breast.

"Why can't we just go back to your place?"

He moved his mouth to my nose and began to suck on it.

"Do you fantasize about fucking on a school grounds?"

I couldn't get a word out of him, so I let him fuck me. It was conveniently warm that night, sticky. While he was inside of me, I began to miss him. He had been tender. He had been electric. I was in so much pain

I began to hurl. Then, I became afraid hurling would hurt his feelings, so I began to moan. When I was moaning, I could tell he liked it, so I began to laugh. I laughed until it was over.

Back at his place, we stretched out on his bed and I sang him to sleep. "Happy birthday to you, happy birthday to you, happy birthday dear Neil, happy birthday to you."

The next morning, I asked him if he missed me, and he told me that he hadn't stopped thinking about me all year. I asked him if he ever loved me, and he said love was such a strange concept. I toured his bedroom to re-familiarize myself. The bed was now pushed to the side of the door. The desk now faced the window. The walls were still covered with the same letters.

"Is it over with Elizabeth now? I heard you guys got back together at the end of last summer."

"Love is such a strange concept," he said again. "I can drive you home. We just need to stop at Shoppers and get you Plan B. I didn't use a condom."

"If I take it—will you stay?"

"Yes."

Back at my place, I took the pill and he got in bed with me. That evening when I woke up, he was gone.

Maggie and I cuddled on our living room floor, staring at the popcorn ceiling, saying nothing at all. There was a dark spot on the ceiling, like a dried puddle—with enough pressure, the ceiling could fall and drown us both.

"I think David's breaking up with me," Maggie said, fighting back a crack cry, gasping for breath. "He said he's feeling depressed, and he needs to work on himself."

The phone rang and it was Neil. It was early in the morning, late at night. A friend of his was on his way to pick me up. He needed to see me and it was urgent. I rolled over and kissed Maggie on the mouth. "Neil needs me," I said.

When we arrived, the house was empty. We went through the backyard, guided by the fire pit, smelling the wet grass. Neil's parents had installed a beautiful campfire last summer. We often sat around it and drank, heard stories of growing up in a multicultural city, of Ted pissing on the tulips in the front porch. This August had been balmy and damp, full of pollen and moisture. I found Neil on the kitchen floor—his vomit spilled on the tiles. I wondered for a minute what it would feel like to lose him permanently. I felt a sense of relief, like, coming out of a burning vehicle and only later realizing it was a burning vehicle.

"Neil? Neil? Neil?" I said, again and again, but

all I got back was the echo of my own voice. I looked behind me and his friend was gone. It was just the two of us again. I reached for him, I pulled on his hair, I lifted his arm.

Neil tossed and rolled over. "What are you doing here?" he said, swinging his arms so hard, he got me on the nose. "Fuck you," he said. He rolled on top of me, bit on my ear. "Sorry," he said. We laid like this for a moment. After some time, ten minutes or so, he rolled on his side and kicked me in the stomach.

I thought about crying, but I had forgotten how. I imagined myself suffocating underneath a mountain of plywood, I imagined myself like a baby bird being driven over, like the roadkill on the streets, like that epic romance blue blues from the movies. But I laid there, next to him, thinking that if I died tonight, it would be an incredibly lonely way to go.

The friend came back and picked me up from the floor. He offered to drive me home, but I insisted on walking. I let myself out from the back door. I walked up to the driveway and sat on the curb. When I moved out of my parents' house, all those months ago, I sat on the grass and hoped my mother would come after me. I waited for an hour—I waited until I knew for certain that nobody would come.

JASMINE SEALY

CAVES

I notice it first in my dreams, the heavy silence. In my dreams we communicate in mute pantomime, our gestures exaggerated like characters in a silent film. You're washing the ceiling, gesturing at the greasy handprints. "How did they get there?" your face seems to ask of me, your eyes bulging. Or maybe, "Are you just going to lie there or are you going to help me?" It's hard to know for sure. Our dreamselves haven't mastered the art of this wordless conversation. I wake feeling as though there is water trapped in my ears.

As if to compensate, my other dream senses are in overdrive, the smells heady, dizzying. Disinfectant, but also guava, the ocean, the dredges of coffee stale on the stove top. We are in the little villa we rented that winter. The one with the bougainvillea bush that shed thorns all over the garden so that we walked across it on tiptoe, a minefield of green. It's the winter I sold my first painting. I'm pregnant with the second baby. You are nesting, standing on one leg on the rattan chair, the sponge dripping bleach onto your face. This is the only way dream-you knows how to prepare, by getting rid of all evidence of what came before. In my dreams it feels as though you are always cleaning. I can't finish a cracker without feeling the hard bristles of the broom at my heels, you sweeping up the crumbs faster than they can hit the floor.

But the dreams don't make sense, the timeline is all wrong. I wouldn't sell my first painting until years later.

We did spend that winter in the villa on the East Coast of the island, that part of the dream is true, but I wasn't pregnant. Not yet, not again. That holiday was after the first miscarriage, the too-long vacation a consolation prize, a "chance for us to reconnect." But once we got to the island you talked of staying. We spent long, uncomfortable days at the beach, the sand hot and itchy, the sand flies nipping at our toes. "Don't you miss this?" you asked, again and again.

Your mother didn't have much time left. You would inherit her house in the island's hilly centre, the bungalow your father built himself. I've seen the pictures of you churning the cement for the bricks, still in a diaper. You have always been rooted to the island in a way I'm not, my family having left all together while I was still a child. But you left alone, an adult already, and now you wanted to come back. To give our child the kind of sun-drenched upbringing you had. Learning to swim in the ocean. Falling out of tamarind trees. Everything was better as you remembered it. More suited to raising our little phantom child. Even the old colonial school system, with its garters and epaulettes, had grown rosy in your memory.

"What would we do here?" I asked.

"Live," you said, "same as anywhere."

But after our month was up, you were ready to leave too. To get back to the city. It would be spring soon, you said, the cherry blossoms would be blooming. Our friends would be having barbeques on their tiny balconies, toasting their craft beers and making summer plans. Could you even find IPA on the island? And was it just you, or did it feel hotter than it had the previous year? And we could always come back to visit, couldn't we? We were lucky in that way, you said, to belong in two places. I didn't feel like I belonged anywhere. I pictured myself then like a fruit bat mid-flight, my body distended, my skin pulled so taut you could almost see through it.

My basement apartment has only one window, facing north, and receives no natural light. It was meant to be temporary, this place. I found it in those cloudy, lost days after you left, and hardly remember visiting before signing the lease. You flew back just to help me move and I remember the feeling of satisfaction I got watching you take it in. The ceiling above the shower permanently wet, spawning mould the only sign of life in the whole place. The mildewed carpet. The dark, damp bedroom. I stood amid my boxes, hands on my hips, daring you to comment.

I could not afford to stay in our old apartment on my own and could not—would not—consider living with roommates. How could I go back to that polite and unintimate form of cohabitation, the tight-throated conversations about who drank the last of the milk, the dancing sock-footed in front of the bathroom, waiting for it to be free? We used to shower together, you and I, and you would piss into the drain while I washed my hair. I went down on you in the kitchen once, toast crumbs cutting my knees, you knocking over the compost bin mid-orgasm, a cascade of banana peels and egg shells. No, I would have to live alone. And this apartment was what I could afford. But you didn't comment, just trekked silently back out to the truck for the next box. Lined our succulents up on the sill of the only window, their leaves already wilting in protest of their new living conditions.

That night, you made us dinner before you left. Noodles in a simple sauce of sherry vinegar and soy and ginger. Stale Oreos for dessert. Afterwards, you washed the dishes, placing the bowls face down on a paper towel. "You need a drying rack," you said. I snaked my arms around your waist and breathed in the space between your shoulder blades. You let me nuzzle there, gasping like a washed-up fish, and then you detangled yourself from my embrace and left before I could ask you to stay. It would take some time before I got used to sleeping underground. That first night, I felt the noodles expanding in my gut, imagined them coming alive and crawling up through my esophagus, out through my nose and ears, then burrowing through the carpet and into the earth.

Now almost a year has passed but I never moved. I used to browse the listings from time to time, but never made any real effort to look for somewhere else. I was hardly home anyway. I spent my mornings painting in the rented studio space I shared with ten other artists, or else sketching in coffee shops, and in the evenings I taught after-school art classes for the local parks department. But now the classes are cancelled, the studio is closed, and so are the coffee shops. No more whiling away the long summer nights on bar patios, no more movies with friends, no more rainy afternoons spent in silent meditation at the gallery, shoulder to shoulder with the other visitors—bored tourists, broke students, broker artists—those willing to brave the line ups for the "by donation" exhibit. All of us breathing in the slow-drying stench of rainwater, shuffling by the paintings like a herd of wet cattle.

That first month in isolation I didn't paint at all. I found there was hardly time, between all the muffins I suddenly felt compelled to bake, applying for unemployment benefits, checking the news, video chatting with friends I hadn't spoken to for years. And when finally I did get my canvas out, the lack of light proved to be a problem. I tried every corner of the apartment, even the bathtub, but beneath the fluorescent bulb the paints became garish, the colours too much like themselves, as though they were showing off. I found I was sickened by all the colour, the screaming whiteness of the white, the petulant blues.

So I put the canvases away, and the paints. One morning I woke to find the clock on the microwave flashing 12:00. The power must have gone off in the night. I glanced at my phone but it was dead. I had no way of knowing the time. I stood on tiptoe and craned my neck to see the small sliver of sky through my half-window. It was a grey strip. I made breakfast without turning any lights on, my eyes adjusting to the near-blackness.

You told me once about an experiment from the sixties, studying the psychological and physical effects of isolation. Two volunteers, a midwife and a carpenter, were left alone in separate caves in the French Alps, lasting eighty-eight days and one hundred and twenty-six days respectively, their only human contact check-ins with the research team, who gave them no information about what was going on beyond the cave. In sunless holes, without clocks, the volunteers sometimes slept for over twenty-four hours at a time and woke to think they'd gone down for only short naps. By the end of the experiment, they'd both lost weeks of time, and were unable to guess accurately how long they'd been in the caves. The strangest part, to me, was that the volunteers estimated they'd been down there for less time than they actually had. Meaning, alone in the darkness, time had passed faster for them than it had for the rest of the world, busying themselves in the light.

On that, my first day of darkness, I lay in bed, the only light the flashing green of my weed vape. I thought about time travel. This was the superpower I'd always longed for, the answer I gave whenever the hypothetical question was raised at dinner parties. You were forever pointing out the flaws, grandfather paradoxes and the like. But I didn't want to go into the past. I didn't want to change anything. I just wanted to fast-forward through my grief like the tired parts of a film I'd seen too many times. This would solve everything. I could take the advice of family and friends and (literally) move on, like an astronaut on an interstellar flight, closing my eyes to the familiar and opening them to a new world.

Even hummingbirds hibernate. I've seen pictures of them dangling like bats from branches, still as death. This, I decided, would be my superpower. If I couldn't travel through time, then I could conquer it entirely, exorcise time from my life like a bad habit. A break from time. It would be like when I quit gluten, only easier. My days were spent in near-torpor anyway. I locked my still-dead phone in my bedside drawer, powered down my laptop and put that away too.

I slept better that first night than I had in weeks, filled with purpose. I thought myself an intrepid researcher embarking on a scientific experiment with profound implications. That was the first night of the silent dreams. I woke, not thinking much of it. I passed another day in timelessness, eating when I was hungry, sleeping when I was tired.

Another day went by. And then another. And now, here I am in the present, with no sense of when that is. I wonder if this is what it feels like to be an infant, before the world imposes its schedules on you, your day shaped only by the needs of your body. You and I had so many plans. I would breastfeed for at least a year. She would be sleep trained at six months and out of diapers before her third birthday. Our child would be a time champion, waking and eating and shitting and sleeping on cue. How foolish we were, to think any of that mattered. If she were here now I would lie with her under the covers, counting her breaths. This would be how I would measure time, in all of the breaths my living child takes while she sleeps soundly beside me.

Some days I don't bother turning on the lights at all, learning instead to navigate the sharp corners of my apartment in the dark. I invent new units of time. Before the nail polish on my pinky toe wore off. Four chapters ago. The third time I flipped the Bob Marley record back to the B side. In the sink, I count seven dirty forks. Has it been a week? I lie in bed and watch as a spider spins a thin web from my dresser to the window. Not much of a web really, just one dangling thread. I am careful not to disturb it as I move around the room. Then, two threads, three. The spider doesn't seem to follow any schedule with her weaving, sometimes abandoning her work for so long I get bored waiting for her to return and go read a book instead. Good for you, I tell her. Time is a construct anyway. She shakes her strange bulbous ass at me but doesn't reply. I need a shower, I say, my last one was three forks ago.

Eventually I run out of food and have to go to the convenience store. I dress up for the occasion, brush my teeth, wash my hair, put on my good tights with no holes, the hoodie that doesn't smell like beef jerky. But when I step outside, the streets are empty, the night tar black and still. Even without a clock I can tell it is the dead of morning, the stores all closed, the windows fogging. I'd thought it was the middle of the day. Back in my apartment, I sit in the dark, my heart thumping. The fridge whines, making those ticking noises I mistook for mice the first few weeks after I moved in. There are other noises too, high-pitched frequencies that seem to radiate from the walls. I feel perverse, as though I've been caught doing something obscene. I have been deluding myself, I realize. I'm no scientist, just a sad woman alone in the dark.

You always said I lacked commitment. That I never paid enough attention to detail—baking starchy cakes because I speed-read the recipe, forever ruining my clothes in half-assed DIY alteration attempts. Even my uterus seemed to lack willpower. "From now on we do it properly," you'd said, after that first year of trying. Yes, yes, yes, I swore to you. I would do everything right. And I did, tracking my cycle in narrow columns in my journal, setting my alarm for three a.m., rolling you on top of me still in half-sleep. "It's time," I'd say, settling you soft and reluctant against my thigh, counting the seconds until you stiffened. I pictured my ovaries like little time bombs, the minutes counting down in flashing red.

I unplug the fridge first. It's empty anyway and I can easily live off dried goods for the duration of the experiment. That helps, but still the apartment hums with electricity. I scour it like a KGB agent looking for bugs. I unplug the Wi-Fi modem, the microwave, all the lamps, the record player and the speakers.

It helps, but it isn't enough. It all just seems wrong somehow, like when you're sitting on the toilet and you catch sight of your own stomach hanging round and hard between your knees and you think *look at me, shitting in this shiny white bowl like that makes me any less of an animal.* All of this stuff, this furniture, the stupid itchy pillows on the couch, the ones that everyone has, with the embroidered flowers. I need to be rid of it all, get down to something true. The crappy carpet, with its bits of old toast and fingernail buried in the pile. The rings of yellow gunk around the bottom of the toilet. The dried snot I flick behind the couch. All the human sheddings, these feel real to me. The succulents, the Febreze, those fucking coasters bought from that pretty fucking shop by the sea. They have to go.

Trappings of life, so they're called. How apt. From *trappe*, the Middle English word for "a cloth for a horse." When was it we decided horses needed clothes and I needed those IKEA cushions, the flowers so universally palatable and yet I tricked myself into thinking I picked them because they meant something, signified some deeper truth about me that I wanted to show the world? Gone, all of it. Into oversized trash bags I leave in piles in the narrow hall. Piles so high I won't be able to leave the apartment without clambering over the heap of black plastic on hand and knee as though scaling a small mountain. No matter. I have nowhere to be.

In the empty room, the furniture all crowded in the middle so it doesn't look like furniture anymore, robbed of its purpose as it is, I can breathe again. The apartment no longer resembles an apartment but rather someone's idea of what an apartment might have looked like, once. Like when I was a child and we went to the museum and stared at the replica hearths of cave men. The woven sheet strewn across the barren stone floor. The whole thing alluding to something like a home, something familiar, but always remaining a bit foreign. We would wonder at the utilitarian emptiness of it all. How did they live like this? My home feels like this to me now. It feels right.

I get out my paints for the first time in weeks and slather the small windowpanes in black. What little light seeped into the apartment before, from the dawning sun or the streetlight down the block, disappears. I light a candle and turn to the bare walls, the plaster speckled and bloated beneath my fingertips. Slowly at first, I run my thickest brush lengthwise, from floor to eye level. I'm not thinking about what to paint, letting the muscles in my forearms make the decisions.

It's been so long since I painted like this, without thought or plan. You were always talking about what the psychologists call "flow," that immersive state of focus, when the days seem to get swallowed up by time, colliding one after the other into the past, without effort, like dominos cascading. You were always downloading apps, signing up for yoga classes, but you never could switch time off the way I could, and you envied me for it. "I called you hours ago," you'd say, waving your phone in front of my face, the call log lit bright and incriminating. "Where do you go," you asked me once, "when you paint?" But I couldn't explain it, still can't. It's the closest I've ever come to my dream of having a superpower, and for months now, it has been lost to me.

My muscles warm up to the task and soon I'm slathering paint onto the walls in long, fluid strokes. In the dim candlelight my work is barely visible, the colours disappearing and reappearing in the shadow. The shapes seem to leap across the walls, alive. "Caves, caves, caves," Alberto Giacometti said, upon encountering the drawings at Lascaux, ". . . there and only there has movement succeeded." The surrealists were nuts for the prehistoric.

Once, when I was in middle school in Toronto, not long after we first arrived in Canada, an art teacher kept me behind after class. She spread my work across her desk like crime scene photos. "What can you tell me about this?" she asked. This was during those early days before I lost my accent, my foreignness making me seem shyer than I was, more malleable. I stumbled for a reply. "I'm sorry," I said, unsure what she was looking for but figuring I'd broken some unspoken rule, another of those mysterious Canadian customs I was still deciphering. On my first day of school I'd jumped the line to board the bus, not realizing that all those people standing politely on the sidewalk were forming a queue. It was the driver who yelled at me, sent me to the back of the line. Since then I'd learned, apologize first, ask questions later.

But I couldn't fathom what possible rule I could have broken in art class. We'd been painting landscapes. I'd copied mine from a postcard gifted to me by my father, from a business trip he'd made to Germany a few years prior. The scene was of a cable car weaving through a green hillside, snowy mountains in the distance. I thought I'd rendered it accurately, down to the small girl who waved at the passing train, her blue hair ribbon rippling in the wind. I remember being very proud of how I'd painted the ribbon, it had seemed at any moment it might catch the wind and blow away from the page.

The teacher stared at the painting as if it caused her great pain to look at. "Where is this scene from?" she asked. I explained the origin of the postcard, and she shook her head, eyes closed, her tight lips curved into a small, sad smile. "But the assignment was to paint a landscape that is familiar to you," she said. "Have you ever been to Germany?" I stammered out a response, explaining how the postcard itself was familiar, how I'd looked at it so many times I could paint it from memory. Of how it spoke to me of that time in my childhood when my father travelled often for work, and my mother and I would always collect him from the airport together, even when his flights landed in the middle of the night. We would sit on the hard benches of the arrivals hall and eat ackees, the green skins falling in a misshapen pile at our feet. And no matter how tired I was, or how long the wait, I was always the first to notice my father as he passed through the sliding doors, an unlit cigarette already dangling from his lips.

The teacher picked up the painting by the corners, as if it were a sodden, smelling bathmat, and tossed it into the trash. "Why don't you try painting a scene from your home country? The beach maybe? Or banana trees?"

Ever since then I have rejected any influence in my work that could ever be mistaken for primitivism. I work in clean lines, muted colours, geometric shapes. Inscrutable images that I like to think of as culturally neutral, as if there is such a thing. But now, in the cave of my creation, I find I'm drawn to the palate I once rejected, filling the walls with great swaths of tropical colour.

That winter we spent in the villa, we used to lie out on the verandah at night, the mosquitoes feasting on our calves, the ocean colliding into the shore, so loud it felt as though at any moment it would suck us out, into its foaming mouth. We were trying to learn the names of the constellations, but the stars were hardly visible. There was a security light on the property that lit the verandah up too bright, and we could never find the switch to turn it off. "You can't see the stars until you turn out the lights," you said, feeling philosophical, high on the local bush weed, half-drunk on rum. We wouldn't talk, only listen, to the ocean, the whistling frogs, the minibus playing its melodic horn on the nearby street. How full the silence was. How much we heard when we stopped trying to fill it.

Now I lie on the dirty carpet of my apartment, the darkness like a warm blanket, and I wonder if you would like it here. There are no stars, but there is a deep and echoing silence the likes of which I have never experienced before. There is no ocean, no nighttime fauna, but there are other sounds, like the slow dripping of my neighbour's toilet, the creaking of the floorboards above me, my own heartbeat, a steady drum. These are real, and beautiful, in their own way.

—

The silence consumes me. Soon it isn't just in my dreams that words begin to disappear. When finally I cannot ignore my own hunger, I venture again to the corner store where the chatty teenager asks about my work while he bags my groceries. He has noticed the paint flecked on my T-shirt, my stained fingertips. I smile at him, nod an apology, gesture to my throat. That first time, he's sympathetic, throws a pack of lozenges into the bag without charging me. But by the third muted shopping trip he looks at me warily. He doesn't ask about the painting anymore or talk to me at all.

Even when I am alone, words fail me. I stare at my own reflection, contorting my mouth into familiar shapes, but no sound comes out. This isn't the first time I've gone mute. That first month after we arrived in Canada, I hardly spoke at all. And then one day I accompanied my mother to the bank where she was to open an account. The teller struggled to understand my mother, though she slowed her speech right down, enunciated each syllable in the RP English she'd been taught in school. After almost half an hour of miscommunication, my mother gave up. She took me by the hand and we left the bank. My mother said we would find another branch. I started school the next day, and when the time came to introduce myself in front of the class all I could picture was that teller, her eyes squinted behind her glasses as she slid a piece of paper across the table, asking my mother to write her questions down instead of speaking them aloud. I mumbled my name and then took my seat at the back of the class. It would be weeks before I spoke again, at the intervention of the school guidance counsellor, who thought I had a learning difficulty.

My mother was furious when she heard. That night after the school contacted her, she had me read aloud from the newspaper after dinner. Every night for weeks I read the paper cover to cover, until I found my voice again.

But this time, I'm comforted by my speechless-ness. It seems to be a sign that the experiment is working, that I am becoming immune to time. Language and time are interconnected, time is abstract, and can only be made real through metaphor. We speak of time using the concrete language of space—a long time, a short time—time experienced as physical distance. Without words, time becomes unbounded, and I sink into it like a warm and bottomless sea. At those depths where no light from the sun reaches, memories

disappear into the sand, or get eaten up by tiny creatures, like the body of some great, decomposing fish.

If I could travel through time, I would mostly use
my powers to skip ahead, but there are some moments
I would like to slow down, to live in again and again.
Like grasping the still-warm corner of a fitted sheet,
watching it billow between us so that for a moment you
disappear, and then, as the sheet falls to the mattress,
here comes: the top of your head, your eyebrows, your
lips. This moment I would suspend in time, stretch it
out like a piece of gum between my fingers, dwell in it
for years, the smell of detergent, you, just on the opposite side of the bed, your face revealing itself to me in
tiny increments.

On one of those nights at the villa, the island heat
sweltering, the air thick and heavy and swarming with
insects, we lay in bed beneath the slow-churning ceiling fan and talked about moving back.

"I want our child to grow up whole," you said,
"I don't want it to have to live like we do, chipping
little bits of itself away to fit in."

"But it wouldn't be like that for her," I argued.
I don't know how I knew the second baby would be a
girl, but I was right, she lived just long enough for us

to find out. "She would be Canadian. She would fit in just fine."

"I want her to know who she is, to know where she comes from."

I wondered then if this is what you thought of me, as a kind of non-person, all the culture seeped out of me like one of those white-on-white modernist paintings I love so much. It was true, I had sanded down my edges, my skin pallid, my accent all but gone. But it hurt to see myself reflected this way in your eyes, and I felt like you were proposing the move back to the island as a test, one that I failed.

I wonder what you'd think of the apartment now, if you could see it. Silent as a vacuum. Paint covering every surface of the walls. Scenes of home—red and fuchsia flowers, white-blue skies, a swirling, frothing sea. And me, arms aching from the effort of it all, my skin speckled, my fingernails thick with colour. "Look," I would tell you, "look what I made." And it would be enough.

ABOUT THE CONTRIBUTORS

Christina Cooke's fiction and non-fiction have previously appeared in *PRISM international*, *The Caribbean Writer*, *Prairie Schooner*, *Epiphany: A Literary Journal*, and elsewhere. A MacDowell Fellow, she holds a Master of Arts degree from the University of New Brunswick and a Master of Fine Arts degree from the Iowa Writers' Workshop. "Homecoming" is an excerpt from her debut novel, *Broughtupsy*, which will be published by Catapult in 2024. Born in Jamaica, Christina is now a Canadian citizen who lives and writes in New York City.

A.Z. Farah is a queer Somali writer who calls Toronto home. Her work is inspired by the folklore and storytelling she heard as a child. She was short-listed for the 2015 Commonwealth Short Story Prize and completed an MFA in creative writing at the University of Guelph. She is currently working on a short story collection about a family of storytellers spinning alternate tales of survival.

Zilla Jones is an African-Canadian woman from Treaty 1 (Winnipeg). She has won *The Malahat Review*'s Open Season Fiction Award, *PRISM international*'s Jacob Zilber Prize for Short Fiction, the gritLIT Festival Short Story Award, and *FreeFall Magazine*'s short prose contest; was the runner-up in the *Prairie Fire* Fiction Contest and *The Puritan*'s Austin Clarke Prize in Literary Excellence; and received an Honourable Mention in *Room* magazine's Fiction Contest. Her stories have been published in *Prairie Fire*, *Room*, *The Puritan*, *Malahat Review*, *PRISM international*, *FreeFall*, and *The Fiddlehead*. She has completed her first novel, *The World So Wide*, set in Grenada during the 1983 American invasion, and is working on her second, *Blackface*, a story about race, identity, police violence, and growing up in the long shadow of colonialism.

Sarah Kabamba's writing has appeared in *Room*, *PRISM international*, *The New Quarterly*, *HA&L Magazine*, *Canthius*, *In/Words Magazine & Press*, *Ottawater*, and *The Vault*. Her work was shortlisted for the 2017 CBC Poetry Prize, longlisted for the 2017 Writers' Trust McClelland & Stewart Journey Prize, and featured in the 2018 edition of Quattro Books' *Best New Poets in Canada* series. She is of Congolese origins and now lives in Ottawa, where she is working on her first collection of poetry.

Born in Congo-Kinshasa, **Téa Mutonji** is a poet and writer based in Toronto. She holds a degree in media studies and minor degrees in English literature and creative writing from the University of Toronto Scarborough. Her debut collection of short stories, *Shut Up You're Pretty*, was the first title from Vivek Shraya's imprint, VS. Books, and named to several best-of-the-year lists, including the *Globe and Mail* and *The Walrus*, among others. *Shut Up You're Pretty* won the 2020 Edmund White Award for Debut Fiction and the Trillium Book Award, and was short-listed for the 2019 Atwood Gibson Writers' Trust Fiction Prize. Téa is the non-fiction editor of *Feel*

Ways: A Scarborough Anthology, published by Mawenzi House. She is the recipient of the 2021 Jill Davis Fellowship in Fiction at NYU.

Born in Canada, with roots in Portland, Jamaica, **Lue Palmer** is a writer of literary speculative fiction, long-form journalism, and poetry. They are a recipient of the 2021 Octavia E. Butler Memorial Scholarship. Their work is focused on Black experiences of nature and climate change, and has been published in the U.S., Canada, and the Caribbean. Lue's first novel, *The Hungry River*, is forthcoming.

Terese Mason Pierre is a writer and editor whose poetry, fiction, and non-fiction have appeared in such publications as *The Walrus*, *The Puritan*, *Room*, *Fantasy Magazine*, and *Quill & Quire*. Her work has been shortlisted for the bpNichol Chapbook Award and nominated for the Rhysling Award, and she is the co-editor-in-chief of *Augur Magazine*. Terese lives and works in Toronto.

Jasmine Sealy is a Barbadian-Canadian writer based in Vancouver, BC. Her short stories and non-fiction have appeared in *The New Quarterly*, *Cosmonauts Avenue*, *Prairie Fire*, *Room*, *Best Canadian Stories 2021*, and elsewhere. In 2017, she was shortlisted for the Commonwealth Short Story Prize, and in 2020 she won the HarperCollins*PublishersLtd*/University of British Columbia Prize for Best New Fiction for her debut novel, *The Island of Forgetting*.

Dianah Smith writes to grieve/retrieve the past, make sense of the present, and leave a legacy for the future. She has been published by the University of Alberta Press, McGraw-Hill Ryerson, the Canadian Centre for Policy Alternatives, the Best of rabble.ca, and *Shameless Magazine*. "The Promise of Foreign" is an excerpt from her novel-in-progress.

Iryn Tushabe is a Ugandan-Canadian writer and journalist. Her creative non-fiction has appeared in *Briarpatch*, *adda*, *Prairies North*, and on CBC Saskatchewan. Her short fiction has been published in *Grain*, *The Carter V. Cooper Short Fiction Anthology Series*, and *The Journey Prize Stories*, and has been shortlisted for the Caine Prize for African Writing. She is currently finishing her debut novel.

ABOUT THE CONTRIBUTING PUBLICATIONS

For more information about the publications that submitted to this year's competition, the Journey Prize, and *The Journey Prize Stories*, please visit www.facebook.com/TheJourneyPrize.

Grain, the journal of eclectic writing, is a literary quarterly out of Saskatchewan that has published engaging and challenging work by Canadian and international writers since 1973. Every issue features new writing from both emerging and established writers and highlights the artwork of a different visual artist. Each fall issue presents the winning stories and poems from our annual Short *Grain* Contest, judged by prominent writers from the Canadian literary community. Additionally, we have established the Kloppenburg Hybrid *Grain* Contest, with the first winners showcased in our Spring 2023 issue. The piece selected from *Grain* for inclusion in this year's *Journey Prize Stories*, "Lucky Baboon" by Iryn Tushabe, was published in our Fall 2020 Short *Grain* Contest issue and won second place (contest judge Casey Plett). Issue editors were Lisa Bird-Wilson (Fiction and Nonfiction) and Alasdair Rees (Poetry). *Grain* is published by the Saskatchewan Writers' Guild, serving a membership in Treaties 2, 4, 5, 6, 8, and 10, which encompasses the unceded territories of the Nêhiyawak, Anishinaabeg, Dakota, Lakota, Nakota, and Dene Nations and the Homeland of the Métis. *Grain* is printed and bound by Houghton Boston in Saskatoon. Editor: Mari-Lou Rowley. Associate Fiction and Nonfiction Editor: Kate O'Gorman. Associate Poetry Editor: Brenda Schmidt. Art Editor/Designer: Shirley Fehr. Correspondence: *Grain* Magazine, P.O. Box 3986, Regina, SK, S4P 3R9. Email: grainmag@skwriter.com Fax: 306 565 8554 Website: www.grainmagazine.ca Twitter/Instagram/Facebook: @GrainLitMag

Founded in 2008 by Emily Schultz and Brian J Davis, **Joyland** is based on the idea that fiction is an international movement supported by local communities. Our editors work with authors globally to highlight the most exciting voices in literary fiction and creative non-fiction. Website: joylandmagazine.com

Maisonneuve publishes and promotes high-quality, original writing on arts, culture, and society. Each article in *Maisonneuve* strives to engage, inform, and inspire. Serving the region of Quebec and its minority anglophone population, as well as a national readership, *Maisonneuve* is uniquely positioned to provide literary, non-main-stream work by emerging and established writers to the Canadian magazine landscape. Submissions can be sent to maisonneuvemagazine.submittable.com/submit.

Prairie Fire is an award-winning Canadian journal of innovative writing that is published quarterly by Prairie Fire Press, Inc. Each issue is a fresh, vibrant mix of fiction, poetry, and creative non-fiction by our most celebrated writers and the hottest new voices of our emerging writers. It consistently features solid writing that will engage your mind and delight your spirit. In a typical issue you will find a wide range of writing, including excerpts from a work-in-progress, a thought-ful essay or memoir, literary humour, lots of poetry and fiction, and sometimes something more experi-mental. *Prairie Fire* has been publishing imaginative, provocative, exceptional, worthwhile writing for over forty years, making it one of Canada's oldest literary magazines. Prairie Fire Press, Inc. is located on Treaty 1 territory, traditional territory of the Anishinaabeg, Cree, OjiCree, Dakota, and Dene Peoples, and on the homeland of the Métis Nation. Website: www.prairiefire.ca

PRISM international is a quarterly magazine out of Vancouver, British Columbia, whose office is located on the traditional, ancestral, and unceded territory of the xʷməθkʷəy̓əm people. Our mandate is to publish the best in contemporary writing and translation from Canada and around the world. Writing from *PRISM* has been featured in *Best American Stories*, *Best American Essays*, and *The Journey Prize Stories*, among other noted publications. *PRISM* strives to uplift and shine a light on emerging and established voices across Canada and internationally and is especially committed to providing a platform for voices who have been systematically marginalized in the literary community, including but not limited to BIPOC groups, cis women, trans women and men, non-binary people, people with disabilities, and members of the LGBTQ2S+ community. Prose Editors: Vivian Li and Tanvi Bhatia. Poetry Editor: Emily Chou. Executive Editors: Emma Cleary and Alison Barnett. Reviews Editor: Eleanor Panno. Submissions and Correspondence: *PRISM international*, Creative Writing Program, The University of British Columbia, Buchanan E462 – 1866 Main Mall, Vancouver, BC, V6T 1Z1. Website: www.prismmagazine.ca

Room, Canada's oldest feminist literary journal, has published fiction, poetry, creative non-fiction, art, interviews, and book reviews for forty years. Published quarterly by the West Coast Feminist Literary Magazine Society, also known as the Growing Room Collective, *Room* showcases writing and art by people of all marginalized genders, including cis and trans women, trans men, non-binary, and two-spirit people. We believe in publishing emerging writers alongside established authors, and because of this, approximately 90 percent of the work we publish comes from unsolicited submissions or contest entries. We accept submissions year-round via Submittable. Website: roommagazine.com

For more than five decades, **This Magazine** has proudly published fiction and poetry from new and emerging Canadian writers. A sassy and thoughtful journal of arts, politics, and progressive ideas, *This* consistently offers fresh takes on familiar issues, as well as breaking stories that need to be told. Publisher: Lisa Whittington-Hill. Fiction Editor: H Felix Chau Bradley. Submissions and correspondence: *This* Magazine, Suite 417, 401 Richmond Street West, Toronto, Ontario, M5V 3A8. Website: www.this.org

Submissions were also received from the following publications:

Augur Magazine
(Toronto, ON)
www.augurmag.com

filling Station
(Calgary, AB)
www.fillingstation.ca

carte blanche
(Montreal, QC)
www.carteblanchemagazine
.com

FreeFall Magazine
(Calgary, AB)
www.freefallmagazine.ca

The Malahat Review
(Victoria, BC)
www.malahatreview.ca

The Fiddlehead
(Fredericton, NB)
www.thefiddlehead.ca

Minola Review
(Toronto, ON)
www.minolareview.com

Riddle Fence
(St. John's, NL)
www.riddlefence.com

Pulp Literature
(Vancouver, BC)
www.pulpliterature.com

SAD Mag
(Vancouver, BC)
www.sadmag.ca

The Puritan
(Toronto, ON)
www.puritan-magazine
.com

Prior to this edition, there was only one Journey Prize winner each year. Beginning with this edition and continuing into future editions, each writer with a story selected for inclusion in the anthology will be considered a Journey Prize winner and will receive $1,000.

* Winners of the $10,000 Journey Prize
** Co-winners of the $10,000 Journey Prize

I

1989

SELECTED WITH ALISTAIR MacLEOD

Ven Begamudré, "Word Games"
David Bergen, "Where You're From"
Lois Braun, "The Pumpkin-Eaters"
Constance Buchanan, "Man with Flying Genitals"
Ann Copeland, "Obedience"
Marion Douglas, "Flags"
Frances Itani, "An Evening in the Café"
Diane Keating, "The Crying Out"
Thomas King, "One Good Story, That One"
Holley Rubinsky, "Rapid Transits"*
Jean Rysstad, "Winter Baby"
Kevin Van Tighem, "Whoopers"
M.G. Vassanji, "In the Quiet of a Sunday Afternoon"
Bronwen Wallace, "Chicken 'N' Ribs"
Armin Wiebe, "Mouse Lake"
Budge Wilson, "Waiting"

2
1990
SELECTED WITH LEON ROOKE; GUY VANDERHAEGHE
André Alexis, "Despair: Five Stories of Ottawa"
Glen Allen, "The Hua Guofeng Memorial Warehouse"
Marusia Bociurkiw, "Mama, Donya"
Virgil Burnett, "Billfrith the Dreamer"
Margaret Dyment, "Sacred Trust"
Cynthia Flood, "My Father Took a Cake to France"*
Douglas Glover, "Story Carved in Stone"
Terry Griggs, "Man with the Axe"
Rick Hillis, "Limbo River"
Thomas King, "The Dog I Wish I Had, I Would Call It Helen"
K.D. Miller, "Sunrise Till Dark"
Jennifer Mitton, "Let Them Say"
Lawrence O'Toole, "Goin' to Town with Katie Ann"
Kenneth Radu, "A Change of Heart"
Jenifer Sutherland, "Table Talk"
Wayne Tefs, "Red Rock and After"

3
1991
SELECTED WITH JANE URQUHART
Donald Aker, "The Invitation"
Anton Baer, "Yukon"
Allan Barr, "A Visit from Lloyd"
David Bergen, "The Fall"
Rai Berzins, "Common Sense"
Diana Hartog, "Theories of Grief"
Diane Keating, "The Salem Letters"
Yann Martel, "The Facts Behind the Helsinki Roccamatios"*
Jennifer Mitton, "Polaroid"
Sheldon Oberman, "This Business with Elijah"
Lynn Podgurny, "Till Tomorrow, Maple Leaf Mills"
James Riseborough, "She Is Not His Mother"
Patricia Stone, "Living on the Lake"

4
1992
SELECTED WITH SANDRA BIRDSELL

David Bergen, "The Bottom of the Glass"

Maria A. Billion, "No Miracles Sweet Jesus"

Judith Cowan, "By the Big River"

Steven Heighton, "How Beautiful upon the Mountains"

Steven Heighton, "A Man Away from Home Has No Neighbours"

L. Rex Kay, "Travelling"

Rozena Maart, "No Rosa, No District Six"*

Guy Malet De Carteret, "Rainy Day"

Carmelita McGrath, "Silence"

Michael Mirolla, "A Theory of Discontinuous Existence"

Diane Juttner Perreault, "Bella's Story"

Eden Robinson, "Traplines"

5
1993
SELECTED WITH GUY VANDERHAEGHE

Caroline Adderson, "Oil and Dread"

David Bergen, "La Rue Prevette"

Marina Endicott, "With the Band"

Dayv James-French, "Cervine"

Michael Kenyon, "Durable Tumblers"

K.D. Miller, "A Litany in Time of Plague"

Robert Mullen, "Flotsam"

Gayla Reid, "Sister Doyle's Men"*

Oakland Ross, "Bang-bang"

Robert Sherrin, "Technical Battle for Trial Machine"

Carol Windley, "The Etruscans"

6

1994

SELECTED WITH DOUGLAS GLOVER;
JUDITH CHANT (CHAPTERS)

Anne Carson, "Water Margins: An Essay on Swimming by My Brother"
Richard Cumyn, "The Sound He Made"
Genni Gunn, "Versions"
Melissa Hardy, "Long Man the River"*
Robert Mullen, "Anomie"
Vivian Payne, "Free Falls"
Jim Reil, "Dry"
Robyn Sarah, "Accept My Story"
Joan Skogan, "Landfall"
Dorothy Speak, "Relatives in Florida"
Alison Wearing, "Notes from Under Water"

7

1995

SELECTED WITH M.G. VASSANJI;
RICHARD BACHMANN (A DIFFERENT DRUMMER BOOKS)

Michelle Alfano, "Opera"
Mary Borsky, "Maps of the Known World"
Gabriella Goliger, "Song of Ascent"
Elizabeth Hay, "Hand Games"
Shaena Lambert, "The Falling Woman"
Elise Levine, "Boy"
Roger Burford Mason, "The Rat-Catcher's Kiss"
Antanas Sileika, "Going Native"
Kathryn Woodward, "Of Marranos and Gilded Angels"*

8

1996

SELECTED WITH OLIVE SENIOR;
BEN McNALLY (NICHOLAS HOARE LTD.)

Rick Bowers, "Dental Bytes"

David Elias, "How I Crossed Over"

Elyse Gasco, "Can You Wave Bye Bye, Baby?"*

Danuta Gleed, "Bones"

Elizabeth Hay, "The Friend"

Linda Holeman, "Turning the Worm"

Elaine Littman, "The Winner's Circle"

Murray Logan, "Steam"

Rick Maddocks, "Lessons from the Sputnik Diner"

K.D. Miller, "Egypt Land"

Gregor Robinson, "Monster Gaps"

Alma Subasic, "Dust"

9

1997

SELECTED WITH NINO RICCI; NICHOLAS PASHLEY
(UNIVERSITY OF TORONTO BOOKSTORE)

Brian Bartlett, "Thomas, Naked"

Dennis Bock, "Olympia"

Kristen den Hartog, "Wave"

Gabriella Goliger, "Maladies of the Inner Ear"**

Terry Griggs, "Momma Had a Baby"

Mark Anthony Jarman, "Righteous Speedboat"

Judith Kalman, "Not for Me a Crown of Thorns"

Andrew Mullins, "The World of Science"

Sasenarine Persaud, "Canada Geese and Apple Chatney"

Anne Simpson, "Dreaming Snow"**

Sarah Withrow, "Ollie"

Terence Young, "The Berlin Wall"

10

1998

SELECTED BY PETER BUITENHUIS; HOLLEY RUBINSKY;

CELIA DUTHIE (DUTHIE BOOKS LTD.)

John Brooke, "The Finer Points of Apples"*

Ian Colford, "The Reason for the Dream"

Libby Creelman, "Cruelty"

Michael Crummey, "Serendipity"

Stephen Guppy, "Downwind"

Jane Eaton Hamilton, "Graduation"

Elise Levine, "You Are You Because Your Little Dog Loves You"

Jean McNeil, "Bethlehem"

Liz Moore, "Eight-Day Clock"

Edward O'Connor, "The Beatrice of Victoria College"

Tim Rogers, "Scars and Other Presents"

Denise Ryan, "Marginals, Vivisections, and Dreams"

Madeleine Thien, "Simple Recipes"

Cheryl Tibbetts, "Flowers of Africville"

11

1999

SELECTED BY LESLEY CHOYCE; SHELDON CURRIE;

MARY-JO ANDERSON (FROG HOLLOW BOOKS)

Mike Barnes, "In Florida"

Libby Creelman, "Sunken Island"

Mike Finigan, "Passion Sunday"

Jane Eaton Hamilton, "Territory"

Mark Anthony Jarman, "Travels into Several Remote Nations of the World"

Barbara Lambert, "Where the Bodies Are Kept"

Linda Little, "The Still"

Larry Lynch, "The Sitter"

Sandra Sabatini, "The One with the News"

Sharon Steams, "Brothers"

Mary Walters, "Show Jumping"

Alissa York, "The Back of the Bear's Mouth"*

12

2000

SELECTED BY CATHERINE BUSH; HAL NIEDZVIECKI; MARC GLASSMAN (PAGES BOOKS AND MAGAZINES)

Andrew Gray, "The Heart of the Land"

Lee Henderson, "Sheep Dub"

Jessica Johnson, "We Move Slowly"

John Lavery, "The Premier's New Pyjamas"

J.A. McCormack, "Hearsay"

Nancy Richler, "Your Mouth Is Lovely"

Andrew Smith, "Sightseeing"

Karen Solie, "Onion Calendar"

Timothy Taylor, "Doves of Townsend"*

Timothy Taylor, "Pope's Own"

Timothy Taylor, "Silent Cruise"

R.M. Vaughan, "Swan Street"

13

2001

SELECTED BY ELYSE GASCO; MICHAEL HELM; MICHAEL NICHOLSON (INDIGO BOOKS & MUSIC INC.)

Kevin Armstrong, "The Cane Field"*

Mike Barnes, "Karaoke Mon Amour"

Heather Birrell, "Machaya"

Heather Birrell, "The Present Perfect"

Craig Boyko, "The Gun"

Vivette J. Kady, "Anything That Wiggles"

Billie Livingston, "You're Taking All the Fun Out of It"

Annabel Lyon, "Fishes"

Lisa Moore, "The Way the Light Is"

Heather O'Neill, "Little Suitcase"

Susan Rendell, "In the Chambers of the Sea"

Tim Rogers, "Watch"

Margrith Schraner, "Dream Dig"

16
2004
SELECTED BY ELIZABETH HAY;
LISA MOORE; MICHAEL REDHILL

Anar Ali, "Baby Khaki's Wings"
Kenneth Bonert, "Packers and Movers"
Jennifer Clouter, "Benny and the Jets"
Daniel Griffin, "Mercedes Buyer's Guide"
Michael Kissinger, "Invest in the North"
Devin Krukoff, "The Last Spark"*
Elaine McCluskey, "The Watermelon Social"
William Metcalfe, "Nice Big Car, Rap Music Coming Out the
Window"
Lesley Millard, "The Uses of the Neckerchief"
Adam Lewis Schroeder, "Burning the Cattle at Both Ends"
Michael V. Smith, "What We Wanted"
Neil Smith, "Isolettes"
Patricia Rose Young, "Up the Clyde on a Bike"

17
2005
SELECTED BY JAMES GRAINGER AND NANCY LEE

Randy Boyagoda, "Rice and Curry Yacht Club"
Krista Bridge, "A Matter of Firsts"
Josh Byer, "Rats, Homosex, Saunas, and Simon"
Craig Davidson, "Failure to Thrive"
McKinley M. Hellenes, "Brighter Thread"
Catherine Kidd, "Green-Eyed Beans"
Pasha Malla, "The Past Composed"
Edward O'Connor, "Heard Melodies Are Sweet"
Barbara Romanik, "Seven Ways into Chandigarh"
Sandra Sabatini, "The Dolphins at Sainte Marie"
Matt Shaw, "Matchbook for a Mother's Hair"*
Richard Simas, "Anthropologies"
Neil Smith, "Scrapbook"
Emily White, "Various Metals"

18
2006
SELECTED BY STEVEN GALLOWAY;
ZSUZSI GARTNER; ANNABEL LYON

Heather Birrell, "BriannaSusannaAlana"*
Craig Boyko, "The Baby"
Craig Boyko, "The Beloved Departed"
Nadia Bozak, "Heavy Metal Housekeeping"
Lee Henderson, "Conjugation"
Melanie Little, "Wrestling"
Matthew Rader, "The Lonesome Death of Joseph Fey"
Scott Randall, "Law School"
Sarah Selecky, "Throwing Cotton"
Damian Tarnopolsky, "Sleepy"
Martin West, "Cretacea"
David Whitton, "The Eclipse"
Clea Young, "Split"

19
2007
SELECTED BY CAROLINE ADDERSON;
DAVID BEZMOZGIS; DIONNE BRAND

Andrew J. Borkowski, "Twelve Versions of Lech"
Craig Boyko, "OZY"*
Grant Buday, "The Curve of the Earth"
Nicole Dixon, "High-Water Mark"
Krista Foss, "Swimming in Zanzibar"
Pasha Malla, "Respite"
Alice Petersen, "After Summer"
Patricia Robertson, "My Hungarian Sister"
Rebecca Rosenblum, "Chilly Girl"
Nicholas Ruddock, "How Eunice Got Her Baby"
Jean Van Loon, "Stardust"

20
2008
SELECTED BY LYNN COADY; HEATHER O'NEILL; NEIL SMITH
Théodora Armstrong, "Whale Stories"
Mike Christie, "Goodbye Porkpie Hat"
Anna Leventhal, "The Polar Bear at the Museum"
Naomi K. Lewis, "The Guiding Light"
Oscar Martens, "Breaking on the Wheel"
Dana Mills, "Steaming for Godthab"
Saleema Nawaz, "My Three Girls"*
Scott Randall, "The Gifted Class"
S. Kennedy Sobol, "Some Light Down"
Sarah Steinberg, "At Last at Sea"
Clea Young, "Chaperone"

21
2009
SELECTED BY CAMILLA GIBB;
LEE HENDERSON; REBECCA ROSENBLUM
Daniel Griffin, "The Last Great Works of Alvin Cale"
Jesus Hardwell, "Easy Living"
Paul Headrick, "Highlife"
Sarah Keevil, "Pyro"
Adrian Michael Kelly, "Lure"
Fran Kimmel, "Picturing God's Ocean"
Lynne Kutsukake, "Away"
Alexander MacLeod, "Miracle Mile"
Dave Margoshes, "The Wisdom of Solomon"
Shawn Syms, "On the Line"
Sarah L. Taggart, "Deaf"
Yasuko Thanh, "Floating Like the Dead"*

22
2010

SELECTED BY PASHA MALLA; JOAN THOMAS; ALISSA YORK

Carolyn Black, "Serial Love"

Andrew Boden, "Confluence of Spoors"

Laura Boudreau, "The Dead Dad Game"

Devon Code, "Uncle Oscar"*

Danielle Egan, "Publicity"

Krista Foss, "The Longitude of Okay"

Lynne Kutsukake, "Mating"

Ben Lof, "When in the Field with Her at His Back"

Andrew MacDonald, "Eat Fist!"

Eliza Robertson, "Ship's Log"

Mike Spry, "Five Pounds Short and Apologies to Nelson Algren"

Damian Tarnopolsky, "Laud We the Gods"

23
2011

SELECTED BY ALEXANDER MacLEOD;
ALISON PICK; SARAH SELECKY

Jay Brown, "The Girl from the War"

Michael Christie, "The Extra"

Seyward Goodhand, "The Fur Trader's Daughter"

Miranda Hill, "Petitions to Saint Chronic"*

Fran Kimmel, "Laundry Day"

Ross Klatte, "First-Calf Heifer"

Michelle Serwatuk, "My Eyes Are Dim"

Jessica Westhead, "What I Would Say"

Michelle Winters, "Toupée"

D.W. Wilson, "The Dead Roads"

24

2012

SELECTED BY MICHAEL CHRISTIE;
KATHRYN KUITENBROUWER; KATHLEEN WINTER

Kris Bertin, "Is Alive and Can Move"

Shashi Bhat, "Why I Read *Beowulf*"

Astrid Blodgett, "Ice Break"

Trevor Corkum, "You Were Loved"

Nancy Jo Cullen, "Ashes"

Kevin Hardcastle, "To Have to Wait"

Andrew Hood, "I'm Sorry and Thank You"

Andrew Hood, "Manning"

Grace O'Connell, "The Many Faces of Montgomery Clift"

Jasmina Odor, "Barcelona"

Alex Pugsley, "Crisis on Earth-X"*

Eliza Robertson, "Sea Drift"

Martin West, "My Daughter of the Dead Reeds"

25

2013

SELECTED BY MIRANDA HILL;
MARK MEDLEY; RUSSELL WANGERSKY

Steven Benstead, "Megan's Bus"

Jay Brown, "The Egyptians"

Andrew Forbes, "In the Foothills"

Philip Huynh, "Gulliver's Wife"

Amy Jones, "Team Ninja"

Marnie Lamb, "Mrs. Fujimoto's Wednesday Afternoons"

Doretta Lau, "How Does a Single Blade of Grass Thank the Sun?"

Laura Legge, "It's Raining in Paris"

Natalie Morrill, "Ossicles"

Zoey Leigh Peterson, "Sleep World"

Eliza Robertson, "My Sister Sang"

Naben Ruthnum, "Cinema Rex"*

26
2014
SELECTED BY STEVEN W. BEATTIE;
CRAIG DAVIDSON; SALEEMA NAWAZ

Rosaria Campbell, "Probabilities"

Nancy Jo Cullen, "Hashtag Maggie Vandermeer"

M.A. Fox, "Piano Boy"

Kevin Hardcastle, "Old Man Marchuk"

Amy Jones, "Wolves, Cigarettes, Gum"

Tyler Keevil, "Sealskin"*

Jeremy Lanaway, "Downturn"

Andrew MacDonald, "Four Minutes"

Lori McNulty, "Monsoon Season"

Shana Myara, "Remainders"

Julie Roorda, "How to Tell If Your Frog Is Dead"

Leona Theis, "High Beams"

Clea Young, "Juvenile"

27
2015
SELECTED BY ANTHONY DE SA;
TANIS RIDEOUT; CARRIE SNYDER

Charlotte Bondy, "Renaude"

Emily Bossé, "Last Animal Standing on Gentleman's Farm"

Deirdre Dore, "The Wise Baby"*

Charlie Fiset, "Maggie's Farm"

K'ari Fisher, "Mercy Beatrice Wrestles the Noose"

Anna Ling Kaye, "Red Egg and Ginger"

Andrew MacDonald, "The Perfect Man for My Husband"

Madeleine Maillet, "Achilles' Death"

Lori McNulty, "Fingernecklace"

Sarah Meehan Sirk, "Moonman"

Ron Schafrick, "Lovely Company"

Georgia Wilder, "Cocoa Divine and the Lightning Police"

30

2018

SELECTED BY SHARON BALA;

KERRY CLARE; ZOEY LEIGH PETERSON

Shashi Bhat, "Mute"*

Greg Brown, "Bear"

Greg Brown, "Love"

Alicia Elliott, "Tracks"

Liz Harmer, "Never Prosper"

Philip Huynh, "The Forbidden Purple City"

Jason Jobin, "Before He Left"

Aviva Dale Martin, "Barcelona"

Rowan McCandless, "Castaways"

Sofia Mostaghimi, "Desperada"

Jess Taylor, "Two Sex Addicts Fall in Love"

Iryn Tushabe, "A Separation"

Carly Vandergriendt, "Resurfacing"

31

2019

SELECTED BY CARLEIGH BAKER; CATHERINE HERNANDEZ;

JOSHUA WHITEHEAD

Sarah Christina Brown, "Land of Living Skies"

Kai Conradi, "Every True Artist"

Francesca Ekwuyasi, "Ọrun Is Heaven"

Jason Jobin, "They Would Pour Us into Boxes"

Hajera Khaja, "Waiting for Adnan"

Ben Ladouceur, "A Boy of Good Breeding"

Angélique Lalonde, "Pooka"*

Michael LaPointe, "Candidate"

Canisia Lubrin, "No ID or We Could Be Brothers"

Samantha Jade Macpherson, "The Fish and the Dragons"

Troy Sebastian/nupqu ʔak‑ɫam̓, "Tax Ni? Pikʼ ak (A Long Time Ago)"

Leanne Toshiko Simpson, "Monsters"

32

SELECTED BY AMY JONES; DORETTA LAU; TÉA MUTONJI

Michela Carrière, "The Moth and The Fox"
Paola Ferrante, "When Foxes Die Electric"
Lisa Foad, "Hunting"
David Huebert, "Chemical Valley"
Jessica Johns, "Bad Cree"*
Rachael Lesosky, "She Figures That"
Canisia Lubrin, "The Origin of Lullaby"
Florence MacDonald, "House on Fire"
Cara Marks, "Aurora Borealis"
Fawn Parker, "Feed Machine"
Susan Sanford Blades, "The Rest of Him"
John Elizabeth Stintzi, "Coven Covets Boy"
Hsien Chong Tan, "The Last Snow Globe Repairman in the World"